'Why not prete

Karin said, her word

'This is insane,' Jed
father of your baby?
around?'

'His lawyers assured me he won't.'

'Calling him a swine or a snake don't seem fair to
the animals,' Jed said, his hands fisting in anger at
his sides. Karin laughed, and suddenly Jed found
himself staring at her mouth and wondering what
it would be like to kiss her. Staring at her hair and
wondering what it would be like to run his
fingers—

He jerked back on his reins and held himself
steady. He had a decision to make. One week and
a little white lie…

Jed gazed into Karin's blue eyes, took her hand in
his. 'If you'll have me as your intended for the
next week, I'd be honoured, ma'am.'

'If you're going to be my husband, maybe you
should stop calling me ma'am…'

Dear Reader,

Take a look at what's in store for you this month:

Baby Boy Blessed from Arlene James is our **That's My Baby!** title and little Georgie apparently has more than a bit of the author's own son in him!

A Royal Baby on the Way comes from Susan Mallery, now a very established writer of Special Editions, and it kicks off an absolutely breathtaking set of five linked books about a royal family with a missing prince. These five books go across Sensation™ & Desire™ as well as Special Edition™, so do keep your eyes open if you want to catch them all—although each book does stand alone!

Cathy Gillen Thacker is back with another of her **McCabe Men** in *His Cinderella*; it's Wade's—the oil millionaire—story.

Three more fantastic books: *Daddy by Surprise* by Pat Warren, *Pregnant & Practically Married* by Andrea Edwards, and *Yours for Ninety Days* by Barbara McMahon complete this month's absolutely stellar line-up.

Enjoy!

The Editors

Pregnant & Practically Married

ANDREA EDWARDS

SILHOUETTE
SPECIAL EDITION®

DID YOU PURCHASE THIS BOOK WITHOUT A COVER?
If you did, you should be aware it is **stolen property** as it was
reported *unsold and destroyed* by a retailer. Neither the author nor
the publisher has received any payment for this book.

*All the characters in this book have no existence outside the imagination
of the author, and have no relation whatsoever to anyone bearing the
same name or names. They are not even distantly inspired by any
individual known or unknown to the author, and all the incidents are
pure invention.*

*All Rights Reserved including the right of reproduction in whole or in part
in any form. This edition is published by arrangement with Harlequin
Enterprises II B.V. The text of this publication or any part thereof may not
be reproduced or transmitted in any form or by any means, electronic or
mechanical, including photocopying, recording, storage in an
information retrieval system, or otherwise, without the written
permission of the publisher.*

*This book is sold subject to the condition that it shall not, by way of trade
or otherwise, be lent, resold, hired out or otherwise circulated without the
prior consent of the publisher in any form of binding or cover other than
that in which it is published and without a similar condition including
this condition being imposed on the subsequent purchaser.*

*Silhouette, Silhouette Special Edition and Colophon are
registered trademarks of Harlequin Books S.A., used under licence.*

*First published in Great Britain 2000
Silhouette Books, Eton House, 18-24 Paradise Road,
Richmond, Surrey TW9 1SR*

© EAN Associates 1999

ISBN 0 373 24283 2

23-1100

*Printed and bound in Spain
by Litografia Rosés S.A., Barcelona*

To all the wonderful people in Chesterton, Indiana, for always making us feel at home when we visit their little bit of Oz.

While Chesterton, Indiana does host a wonderful Wizard of Oz Festival each year, the authors have taken some liberty with the history and actual events of the festival.

ANDREA EDWARDS

is the pseudonym of Anne and Ed Kolaczyk, a husband-and-wife writing team who have been telling their stories for more than fifteen years. Anne is a former primary school teacher, while Ed is a refugee from corporate America. After many years in the Chicago area, they now live in a small town in northern Indiana, where they are avid students of local history, family legends and ethnic myths. Recently they have both been bitten by the the gardening bug, but only time will tell how serious the affliction is. Their four children are grown; the youngest attends college, while the eldest is a college professor. Remaining at home with Anne and Ed are two dogs, four cats and one bird—not the same ones that first walked through their stories but carrying on the same tradition of chaotic rule of the household nonetheless.

(BEEP): Hi, Mum, it's me, Karin. I just got your message about finding that box of memorabilia from my old school club, The Bridal Circle. Remember when my girlfriends and I used to plan our perfect weddings? Anyway, I've given up on the perfect wedding—or any wedding, for that matter. Recycle it, will you?

Can't wait to see you, Mum, and the old home town. But, please, please, don't try to fix me up on a date while I'm home.

Maybe I should warn you now…I've got a humdinger of a surprise. Are you sitting down? How do you like the sound of *Grandma?* See you soon—love you!

Prologue

Karin rolled over in her sleeping bag and stared out through the screen door at the moonlit farmyard. The lights were out in the family room, and the four girls were all stretched out in their sleeping bags. Penny, Heather and Dorothy were asleep but Karin was still wide awake. Wide awake and irritated.

The best part of Penny's slumber party was over and they'd never told the ghost stories Karin had wanted to tell. No, instead they'd spent hours planning their stupid weddings.

That had been the biggest waste of time ever. They were in high school and none of them even had a real boyfriend, so what was the big deal?

"Karin, are you awake?" Dorothy whispered.

Karin rolled back over. Dorothy's sleeping bag was right next to hers, and even in the darkness she could see that Dorothy's eyes were open.

"I thought you were asleep."

Dorothy shook her head. "I ate too much popcorn. If I go to sleep now, I'm going to have nightmares."

"I'm going to have them from all that wedding talk," Karin said. "I had the greatest ghost story I wanted to tell, too."

Dorothy scooted a little closer. "You can tell me."

Karin hesitated. The right mood for a ghost story had passed. Besides, she wanted to scare all three of her friends. "Maybe I'll keep it until next time."

"Okay."

Dorothy rolled over on her back and was silent a long time. So long that Karin thought maybe she'd fallen asleep, but then she turned to Karin.

"Why didn't you like planning our weddings?" she asked. "I would have thought…"

Karin sighed. "That I'd have all sorts of plans because I've been to so many?" she finished for Dorothy. "Maybe that's just it. I've been to too many. The next time my mom gets married, I think I'll skip it. Hey, it's not like I won't have the chance to see her get married again in a few years."

"I like your mom," Dorothy said.

Karin took her turn at being silent, then sighed again. She shouldn't have spoken that way. It sounded mean, as though she didn't care about her mother. "I like her, too. It's those jerks she marries that I don't like. Men are jerks and cowboys are scum."

"Don't say that," Dorothy whispered, half raising herself on her elbow. "You know it's not true. One day you're going to marry a wonderful man and you'll see that it's not."

Karin looked at the ceiling. "The only way I'm going to my wedding is on a team of wild horses," she said. "I'm not ever going to fall for that love non-sense."

"Never's a long time," Dorothy said.

"Not nearly long enough."

"Would you two go to sleep?" Penny said from across the room, her voice groggy with sleep.

Dorothy lay back down and Karin turned to stare out the screen door. Her friends could make all the romantic plans for weddings they wanted to, but she wasn't going to. She was never ever getting married because she was never ever falling in love.

It wasn't just because she didn't want to, but also because she didn't think she could. She'd loved Hadley, her stepfather when she was six, but that hadn't stopped him from making her and her mom both cry all the time. When her mom married Wally, the stepdad that came next, Karin let herself like him but she didn't cry when he left, and she didn't bother to like the stepfathers that came later. Liking someone was okay, unless you liked them too much. Then it was dumb. Loving someone was just plain idiotic.

She never had crushes on kids at school, thought Valentine's Day was a waste of time and hated mushy TV shows and movies. She didn't care if the kids at school said she had no heart, it was much better that way. No one would ever hurt her again.

Chapter One

"It'll just be a minute more." The young woman at the airport glanced briefly at the car-rental form the printer was spitting out, and flashed a warm smile Jed's way. "Are you going to be in town for a while?"

He stared at her a long moment. It was only a little harmless flirting—something he used to be good at, and then good at fending off after he and Wendy had gotten married. But since her death last year, the whole idea of flirting left him cold.

"No, ma'am," he said crisply. "We're just passing through Chicago."

"What a shame." Her voice was more than a little inviting. She tore the form from the printer, putting it on the counter as she held out a pen. "If you'll sign at the bottom, you and your little girl—"

The woman stopped speaking, her gaze suddenly off Jed and onto Lissa. Jed glanced down at his daughter.

Damn, she'd taken off her sunglasses and her trade-mark big brown eyes were visible for everyone to see—and recognize. With a laugh that he hoped masked the fact he had no more air in his lungs, he turned back to the clerk.

"My heavens," she was murmuring. "I just noticed. She looks exactly like that cereal girl on TV."

"Yeah, we hear that a lot," he said quickly and scribbled his name on the line. "Can't see it myself though. Where'd you say we catch the shuttle to the parking lot?" He took a step to one side, blocking her view of Lissa.

The woman seemed to shake herself then smiled a more businesslike smile. "Just step through that door there and wait by the yellow sign. A courtesy bus will be along soon to take you to your car."

He tried for a bit of the McCarron charm, flashing that lopsided grin that had left the ladies happy when he'd been on the rodeo circuit. "Thanks." He grabbed the handle of the luggage cart and Lissa's hand and hurried toward the exit.

"Put your sunglasses back on, darlin'," he told his daughter under his breath. "Now."

"She was very pretty," Lissa pointed out as she put the glasses back on. "And we aren't in any rush."

"She recognized you."

"I bet she would have liked to have lunch with us."

Jed sighed as they went out into the warmth of mid-September in Chicago. A car-rental bus pulled away from the marked stop. Oh well, another would be along in a few minutes. Buses were one of the things in life that you could miss and count on another coming along.

"Why didn't you call her darlin'? You used to call all the ladies darlin' and now it's only me."

Jed frowned at his daughter. "The other ladies might not understand," he said. "It's just a word, and they might think I was interested in something more serious."

"Mommy wouldn't want you to be alone."

"I'm not. I have you."

"Daddy." There was a hint of his Oklahoma drawl in her voice. "I'm growing up. I'm going to be leaving for college soon. And after that, I'll be going to South America to save the rain forests. You have to find some friends of your own."

"You're eight. I've got time."

"Not at the rate you're going."

He frowned at the darkening clouds, then stared down the bus lanes trying to see if another was coming, but the road was empty.

"Besides," Lissa went on. "You're getting older and that's going to make it even harder for you to find friends."

He fought the urge to point out he was only thirty-five—hardly over the hill—but he was not going to let Lissa distract him. He might not have mastered French braids yet, but he had learned Lissa was an expert at bait and switch.

"Look, you wanted to vacation like a regular kid," he reminded her. "Without any Crunchy Flakes PR people handing out autographed pictures and security people holding back the crowds. I agreed to it, even though you're missing school, but only if you'd stay unobtrusive. That meant sunglasses, dresses and a hat."

"I hate sunglasses, and dresses are for sissies."

Jed glanced around them. A couple had joined them at the bus stop but they had eyes only for each other. Jed looked away, his jaw tightening suddenly. He'd had that kind of love once, and never would again. One love to a customer and he'd lost his. He took a deep breath that brought him a lungful of exhaust fumes, but also some sanity.

"Dresses are fine," he told Lissa. "Girls wear dresses all the time."

"I don't."

No, she didn't. Not in real life and not in the Crunchy Flakes commercials. That's why he'd suggested dresses. As the Crunchy Flakes official spokesperson for the last two years, Lissa always wore jeans in the ads—her own designer label, "Lissa's Line," which were sold at better department stores. So a dress would be a different look. And the Crunchy Flakes people tinted her blond hair a brownish red and curled it into a riot of corkscrews that could barely be contained into two pigtails—so Jed had washed the tint out and combed her hair back into a ponytail for their vacation. There was no way to hide those big brown eyes though—except with sunglasses. And she was going to keep those on. He was not going to risk Lissa being mobbed by fans and maybe hurt in the process. Not like that time in Albany when she'd been honorary chairperson of the Reading Adventure Program.

"Here comes the bus," Jed said, grateful to see another yellow vehicle coming around the bend. "Pick up your bag."

Lissa wrinkled her nose at him but she did as she was told. Would she do that as a teenager or would she fight him every step of the way? He'd been in some tough situations in his youth on the rodeo circuit, but none of them were as hard as being a widower and a single father.

The bus pulled up to the curb and they hopped on. He put their suitcases in the carrying rack, and tossed in Lissa's overnight bag before taking a seat next to her. She was kneeling on the seat looking back at the airport terminal, her whole body alight with excitement and energy.

Jed sat back in the seat, a weary kind of contentment settling over him as he watched her. She had such a zest for life. Everything she did was an adventure that she shared with those around her. She just radiated enthusiasm until everyone fell under her spell.

He and Wendy hadn't planned on Lissa becoming a celebrity. In fact, if they could have looked into the future, Jed wasn't sure they would have agreed to her making that first commercial. They never dreamed that within months Lissa would be the featured spokesperson for the breakfast cereal, with guest spots on television shows and her own fan club. Or that a year later, Wendy would be gone.

"We're here, Dad."

Jed slowly pulled himself back to the real world, his eyes sweeping the lines of cars filling the rental-company parking lot. He didn't see anybody that looked like a reporter. In fact, he saw few other people. They could get their car and quickly be on their way to Chesterton.

"What kind of car are we getting?" Lissa asked.

"A blue sedan."

Lissa made a face. "Dad, that's a geezer car."

"It'll get us where we want to go," he said.

"So would a Jeep."

Jed led the way off the bus. Lissa followed him.

"And if it snowed, the Jeep would be a whole lot safer."

"It doesn't snow in Indiana in September."

"It could." She hurried to catch up with him. "It might not, but it could. I mean, we are going to northern Indiana, aren't we?"

"It won't," Jed said. "I guarantee it."

"You can't do that."

Lissa was right. He couldn't guarantee a damn thing. If he could, he would have guaranteed that drunk drivers stayed off the highways and that mothers lived a long time so that daughters were never alone. He would have guaranteed that the worst sorrow Lissa would have had to face growing up was not having pizza for dinner every night of the week.

"Daddy?"

He took hold of himself and clamped down on the darkness. Shut it off, locked it up, turned his back on it. He was not feeling it, none of it.

"You're right, darlin'," he said briskly. "We don't want some tame old blue sedan. I'll change this to something exciting. Maybe a Road Ranger."

"No." She pulled at his hand. "Come on, let's get our car and get going. If we hurry, maybe we can get to Chesterton before it rains."

His stomach tightened as he looked into her face. The child psychologists he'd consulted after Wendy's death had told him that losing a parent was traumatic enough for a child, that he shouldn't change anything else in Lissa's life. That she should continue in the same school and as the Crunchy Flakes little darling. So he'd quit the rodeo circuit and got a job with an animal trainer in Hollywood, working regular hours so he could be there for her.

He didn't miss the rodeo life; it had only been a source of income. And since his dream of buying a little ranch and raising horses had died along with Wendy, he didn't need that much income anymore. No, all he needed was for Lissa to heal, and that seemed to be a slow process.

But when he'd suggested a vacation she'd really lit up, spilling out this whole dream. She didn't want to go to Walt Disney World or Hawaii. Nope, just Chesterton, Indiana's Wizard of Oz Festival.

She wanted to eat dinner with the Munchkins, watch the parade of Oz characters and follow Dorothy and Toto around the town in the traveling production of *The Wizard of Oz*. She wanted to enter the costume contest and walk through town on the Yellow Brick Road.

Wendy had spent two years in northern Indiana when her dad was the army recruiter in Valpariso, and some of her happiest childhood memories had been of the Oz festival in nearby Chesterton. Lissa remembered every single story Wendy had told of the place and had plans to relive them all. So, was vacationing in Chesterton going to help Lissa heal or hurt her more if it didn't match up to her expectations?

Jed stopped next to their car and looked up at the gathering storm clouds. They seemed prophetic, an omen of trouble ahead.

"It's not too late to change our minds," he said. "We could head north to the Wisconsin Dells and go boating."

"No, thank you." She pulled open the back door of the sedan and tossed her bag in. "Besides, I want to talk to Glinda."

Jed threw the larger bags into the trunk, then got in

the driver's side as Lissa got in the car. "Who's Glinda? We don't know anybody in Chesterton."

Lissa rolled her eyes as she leaned her head against the seat back. "Glinda, the Good Witch of the South, Dad."

"Huh?"

She just shook her head. "She's the one who helps the Scarecrow get back to Emerald City," Lissa explained. "And the Tinman back to the Winkies and the Lion back to his forest. Then she tells Dorothy how to get home. You never read *The Wizard of Oz,* did you?"

"Uh, no." He pulled the car out of the parking space, a little worry creeping into his soul. "So why do you want to talk to Glinda?"

But Lissa just turned to stare out the window as if the exit ramp from the car-rental garage was the most fascinating thing in the world. "This is going to be the best vacation ever," she said. "I just know it."

Karin Spencer stared out the restaurant window, watching the black clouds grow more menacing by the moment. The sun had long since disappeared, leaving the tollway oasis looking even more bleak and depressing.

"Oh, cool. Looks like we're in for a storm."

Karin turned to find a waitress at her side. The woman was smiling and cheerful. It was enough to make Karin cringe inwardly. Lately, the sun didn't even begin to chase her shadows away. A whole galaxy probably couldn't lift her spirits, so a little storm shouldn't bother her.

"So what'll you have?" the waitress asked. "We've got a special on fried chicken. All you can eat. Or we've got some freshly made Dutch apple."

Oh, yuck. The very idea of food had Karin's stomach churning. She swallowed hard. "Decaffeinated tea," she said. "And whole wheat toast."

The woman stared at her for a long moment as if Karin was some sort of alien, then scooped up the menu. "Okay. Coming right up."

As the woman hurried away, Karin closed her eyes and sank back in her chair. Was it the smell of the fried chicken or the idea of apple pie? Or maybe the words *all you can eat?*

Most likely it was because she'd skipped breakfast. Whatever it was, she should never have stopped here. She should just have kept on driving, getting off the toll road at the Chesterton exit. If she'd done that, she wouldn't be sick now.

She opened her eyes. Actually, she never should have gotten on the toll road. In fact, she should never have left her Lake Shore Drive apartment. But if she really hadn't wanted to be sick, she should never have gone to bed with a scumbag like Dr. Rico Swanson. Or since it had been her own stupidity that let her be swayed by his smile, at least she should have made sure she wouldn't get pregnant. Fat lot of good her medical degree had done her.

But it was too late now. Too late to realize Rico had just been a pathetic attempt to prove she could love. Too late to turn down the honor of dressing up in that Glinda costume and being grand marshal of the Oz festival next weekend. Too late to tell Penny and Brad she couldn't come to the wedding. Too late to tell her mother that something had come up. And, given the definite five-month-size bump in her belly, too late to tell people everything was just fine and dandy. At least in this baggy dress, maybe she could get through the week without *everybody* knowing.

"Look, Daddy. It's Glinda!" a child's voice said.

Karin froze, her whole body quaking in horror at the idea of it starting already, but then sanity returned and she twisted slightly. The girl was looking at a poster for the Oz festival. It had been silly to think it was anything else. That frilly pink dress Glinda was wearing in the picture was in her friend Heather's closet along with the magic wand and rhinestone crown. And Karin was about as far from a wise and powerful witch as she could be, so no one would look at her and think Glinda. The Tinman maybe, but not Glinda.

"Glinda sure is pretty," the man was saying. "What was it you wanted to ask her?"

The little girl's laughter danced in the air. "That's a secret, Daddy. Just between me and her."

Karin found herself staring at the girl, at her straight blond ponytail and the dress that seemed too frilly for the energy vibrating in the air around the girl. No, it was more than energy. It was hope and confidence and certainty. About what? That Glinda would be able to answer her mysterious question?

Another weight fell onto Karin's shoulders, this one just too much. She jumped to her feet, digging in her purse for some money.

"Hey, honey. Where you going?" The waitress was there with her toast and tea.

"I have to go," Karin said and tossed a few dollar bills onto the table. "That should cover it."

"Go where?" the waitress asked.

"You can't go anywhere," the little girl's father said.

Karin looked at him then. Really looked at him. Tall.

Athletic. Good-looking with tan features. A cowboy, right down to the hat and boots.

He was every mother's dream for their daughter. Or at least, Karin's mother's dream for her. What had her mother done—picked out her cowboy and sent him to the toll road to look for her?

"There's a bad storm coming," the little girl said, pulling off her sunglasses and smiling at Karin with her big brown eyes. "Daddy said it's not safe outside."

Karin looked at the cowboy again, almost drowning in the brown eyes that were a mirror of his daughter's. But was it safe inside them?

She shook off the insane question and turned back to smile at the girl. If the cowboy was Daddy, it meant Mommy was around. So this guy was just a guy. And the little girl was luckier than Karin had ever been.

"I'll be fine," she told them. "I don't mind a little rain."

"That's more than a little rain," the waitress said, picking the money up off the table before leaving.

"There were all sorts of severe weather warnings on the radio," the cowboy pointed out. "It's not safe to drive out there."

Who made him emperor? Karin glanced out the window and, before she could look away, saw he was right. It was pouring, the rain coming down almost sideways from the force of the wind. Still, she didn't need—or want—some man telling her what to do.

"I'm used to these storms," she told him. "I grew up here."

"You did?" The girl looked as though she'd forgotten the storm and climbed onto one of the chairs at Karin's table, hanging an overnight bag over the back. "My mom used to live around here too when she was in fifth grade. Did you know her? Her name was Wendy McCarron.''

"It was Wendy Shapiro then," the cowboy corrected gently. "And this is a big area, Lissa. I doubt that this lady would have known her."

For some unexplainable reason, Karin felt as if she was letting them down. But the name meant nothing. "I'm sorry, I don't think I did."

"That's okay." The girl shrugged. "She died last year but she had a good time when she lived here. That's why we're going to the Oz festival."

"She died? Oh, I'm so sorry." Karin felt doubly awful. Why hadn't she said she'd known the little girl's mother, liked her, thought of her often? A compassionate person would have known to lie. Just more proof that the kids had been right all through school—she didn't have a heart.

"No problem," the cowboy said. "We're doing okay. What do you say we find ourselves a table and have some lunch, Lissa?"

His voice had an edginess that said no trespassing. That walls were in place to protect him and his Lissa and no one was getting by them. Not that Karin was inclined to try. His type of heart troubles weren't the type she could fix with a scalpel.

"Well, I do hope you have a wonderful time at the festival." Karin picked up her raincoat. "And take this table. I'm going."

"You can't," the girl cried. "This is just like Dorothy's storm. A tornado could lift up the restaurant and dump it back down on you."

"Lissa, that's not going to happen," the man said gently. He stooped down and took his daughter's hands in his, even as he flashed a sharp glance Karin's way. "No one's going out in the storm just now."

A jumble of reactions tugged at her. Annoyance that he was ordering her around. Concern that the girl was worrying over her. And something else that caused a stinging in her eyes and an emptiness in her stomach.

Maybe it was just more indigestion. Maybe it was just worry about the upcoming week in Chesterton. Or maybe it was the knowledge that her child wouldn't have a father to comfort her when she got scared.

Karin sucked in a deep steadying breath. And so what if her baby wouldn't? Karin had grown up without a father and she had done fine. She was a leading cardiac surgeon in Chicago, able to command huge fees for her services. Anything her baby needed, she could buy.

She clutched her raincoat to her thickened waistline as if it would keep her child from seeing what it would never have.

"Actually, I meant I was going to the ladies' room," Karin told Lissa. "The storm will probably be gone by the time I get out."

The storm outside, maybe. The storm that was her life—never.

"Do you think that lady will leave while it's raining?" Lissa asked.

Jed lowered his menu. "I'm sure she'll be careful." Though even as he said the words, he realized he was splitting hairs. Being careful didn't necessarily mean that dark-haired beauty would stay in the building. He tried to remind himself that the woman was an adult and free to make her own decisions, but all he kept seeing was that wary look in her eyes. He tried to push it away, and push away the memory of seeing that same look in animals afraid to trust.

It wasn't his problem. She wasn't his problem. And it was just coincidence that he'd chosen the chair facing the door to the ladies' room. He was not getting involved.

"So what are you going to have for lunch?" he asked Lissa.

"She was pretty," Lissa said.

Jed frowned. "Yes, she was," he said.

Wendy had been a blonde, like Lissa. Sunshine and laughter and cascading yellow roses on the bush by the back door. That woman was a midnight thunderstorm. Violets blooming in secret on the forest floor. And eyes as forbidding as an icy mountain lake.

Damn. Where had all that come from?

He shook his head and stared at the menu again. "I'm going to try the fried chicken."

"I think she was scared, too."

"Maybe storms make her nervous." He put down the menu and glanced around for the waitress. The place was packed. It looked as if everybody had pulled in to wait out the storm.

"She looked like that dog you rescued last winter," Lissa said. "You remember, that big white one that wouldn't let anybody come near him."

He brought his gaze back to Lissa with a sigh. "Lots of people don't trust easily. Did you decide what you're going to have?"

"I don't know. Maybe—"

The dark-haired woman came out of the ladies' room, skirting a crowd lingering by the pay phones. She looked pale and held herself tightly as if trying to shield herself from some unseen danger, but her head was high, too. For some reason, he was seeing Joan of Arc. Or an early Christian marching into the Colosseum in Rome. As he watched, she marched across the lobby and headed straight for the wide expanse of plate-glass windows and doors where the calm had disappeared and the wind was picking up with a roar. She was leaving.

Damn.

Jed leaped to his feet.

"Daddy?" Lissa said, then her breath caught as she turned around. "Oh, Daddy, stop her!"

He was halfway across the restaurant, but the woman had a good lead on him. He broke into a run. The people who had been leaving had changed their minds and were standing around. In the way.

"Hey!" someone protested when he bumped them.

"Watch it," someone else cried.

He just kept on going. This was insane, he knew. Totally crazy. This woman was nothing to him, nothing to Lissa. Just a chance encounter. She had the right to do what she pleased, even if that meant taking a risk like driving in a storm.

But Lissa had taken a liking to her, and seeing the woman in danger wasn't the way for Lissa's vacation to start.

Hell, it wasn't the way for his to start, either. He'd analyze his actions later, now there was only time—

"Ma'am!" he cried.

She pushed open the first of the double doors.

"Darlin', wait."

She was a half step from the outside door, but he was right behind her and grabbed her arm.

She swung around, her face angry. "What are—"

As she turned toward him, the roar outside exploded

into a deafening rage. He heard a crash near him, then another and then the row of newspaper vending machines blew over, skidding across the sidewalk in a horrendous screech. A trash can flew into the door but somehow the glass held.

The woman screamed and turned back into him. It was rodeo time—react fast and think later. In one quick movement, he scooped her up into his arms and pulled into the building just as the sign atop the doorway came crashing down, breaking the plate-glass doors and windows. Glass and debris flew everywhere.

He kept moving away from the doors even as he felt the woman go limp in his arms. Finally beyond the glass and the wind, he looked down at the pale beauty. Her eyes were closed, her breathing shallow.

''Somebody call 911,'' he shouted. ''Now!''

Chapter Two

"Is she dead?" Lissa asked, her voice a worried whisper.

Jed carried the woman away from the doorway and all the glass and debris. "No, darlin'. She's gonna be just fine. Want to spread that raincoat on the floor for the lady to lie on?"

Lissa quickly spread the coat out in front of a soda vending machine and Jed laid the woman down gently. Holding her up against him, he'd been able to feel her heart beating, but now he had to look closely to see the gentle rhythmic movement of her chest. He could feel a crowd gathering around them and looked up, hoping for a doctor, but no one seemed ready to take over.

"Is she okay?" the waitress asked.

"Damn, but she's lucky," an old man said.

"She owes this cowboy her life," someone else said.

But Jed was barely listening. He'd done some simple doctoring on the rodeo circuit, but always to other hardheaded cowboys. Never to a pale, fragile beauty. He knelt at the woman's side and leaned over her, touching her cheek softly.

"Come on, darlin'," he said so only she could hear. A baby was crying someplace nearby, and all around them people were talking—yelling—but he closed out all the noise and hubbub. "You can't be done fighting with me yet, darlin'. Open up those pretty blue eyes."

As he spoke, she stirred slightly, turning her head with a soft moan. Her right hand fluttered slightly, like a bird with a broken wing.

"I think she's waking up, Daddy," Lissa told him, dropping her overnight bag next to him as she knelt on the edge of the coat.

Jed stayed bent over the woman, kept on talking in that same soft voice. "Just open those eyes now."

Her hand fluttered again and he took it in his. She clutched him back, sending ripples of warmth down his arm that he had to force himself to ignore. He tried to find reassurance in the strength of her grip, but she still wasn't waking up.

"Maybe she's in a coma," the old man said.

"I heard people can be in comas for years and years," someone else said. "She might never wake up."

Jed glared at the man who was speaking. "Somebody want to get me a damp cloth?" Jed asked. "And how about a glass of water?"

Lissa sat back on her heels, watching as the waitress and an older man hurried off. "You think she's thirsty, Daddy?" she asked.

"I think people needed a way to help." He smiled

at his daughter so serious and worried, then turned back to the woman, brushing the dark hair from her face. A thin trickle of blood had been hiding under her hair. Damn. The little lady had taken a whack to the head.

He glanced up for a moment to listen to sounds in the distance, then back down. "Help's coming, darlin'. Hear those sirens? They'll be here in less time than it'd take a Brahma bull to toss me."

He squeezed the woman's hand a little tighter but her grip didn't change and he couldn't help but frown as he stared into the woman's face. Her dark hair spread out over the cream color of her coat. His heart trembled before he told it to be still. It was just that she looked so very fragile.

"Here, honey, here's a damp towel." The waitress handed the damp cloth to Lissa. "You wash her face a little. Your daddy can't let go of her."

"I don't have to." Jed took the towel from Lissa in his free hand and wiped away the trickle of blood, then pressed the cool cloth to the woman's temple. A little color returned to her cheeks.

"Why can't Daddy let go of her?" Lissa asked.

"Because," the waitress said. "He's pouring the life force from his soul into hers. It's how she maintains contact with this world."

He made a face at Lissa, telling her not to believe all this, but she wasn't looking at him. She was staring at his hand clutching the woman's. As if she was seeing the force, the energy, the power go from him into the stranger. Which was all hogwash, of course.

But was it his imagination or was more color returning to the woman's cheeks?

The old man came back with the water but there wasn't much for Jed to do with it. If this had been a cowboy, Jed might have thrown the water into his face to wake him up. Where the hell was that ambulance?

"You know, she looks like Snow White, Daddy," Lissa said slowly. "Maybe you should kiss her."

"Kiss her?" Jed's heart practically stopped. But at the same time, his eyes were drawn to the woman's lips, almost against his will. Certainly against the advice of his head. "I can't kiss her."

"You have to," Lissa argued. "That's how the prince helped Snow White wake up."

"Well, I'm not a prince." He shifted his weight off his bad knee as if it would shift everyone's attention somewhere else. "I'm just an ex–rodeo cowboy."

"You saved her life," someone pointed out.

"You're on your knees in front of her."

"That's all stuff princes do," someone else said.

Prince Charming. Prince of a fellow. Prince-brand spaghetti. Jed took a deep breath to get his scattered thoughts back in place. They reassembled reluctantly and he went back to his cowboy doctoring. Pressing the wet cloth to her forehead and cheeks, squeezing her hand.

"Where's the ambulance anyway?" he muttered. "Hang in there, darlin', help's a comin'."

"Daddy, she needs a kiss," Lissa pressed. "Just a little one."

He was getting worried that the woman wasn't coming to. She really should have by now, but a kiss wasn't going to help. She needed medical treatment, not a fairy-tale remedy. Still, what would it hurt?

He leaned down and brushed her lips with his. It could hardly even be called a kiss. There was no pressure, no lingering, no dancing of souls on the edge of ecstasy.

No awakening, either. He sat back on his heels, conscious of a tingling in his lips even so. It was just worry or embarrassment, but he could feel the tingling spread a slow warmth through him.

"Darn," Lissa said sadly. "It was supposed to wake her up."

He hadn't been asleep so it couldn't have woken him up. "It was a long shot," he admitted. "But here's the ambulance."

It had just rolled into view, planting itself in the opening where a plate-glass window had once been. Jed gratefully watched as three attendants, two men and a woman, came hurrying into the building.

"Move back, please. Move back," the female paramedic said as she pushed her way through the small crowd. The paramedic plunked a medical bag down and dropped to her knees, but she barely had room to open it. "Come on, people. Let's give the lady a little room."

They backed off a little more but Jed only moved enough to make room for Lissa to come around next to him. The woman was still clinging to his hand and he had no urge to pull himself free. They were wrong about this life-force stuff and certainly wrong that he had saved the woman's life, but he wasn't taking any chances.

"She get hit by debris?" the paramedic asked.

"I don't know," Jed said. "I tried to pull her away from the door and she collapsed. She's got a cut by her hairline."

The paramedic had slipped a blood-pressure cuff around the woman's arm, and was listening to her heart. Once she pulled the tips of the stethoscope from her ears, Lissa's worries spilled out.

"She's gonna be okay, isn't she?" Lissa whispered to the paramedic. "We don't want anything to happen to her. Daddy's her prince."

"Lissa," Jed cautioned. She shouldn't be saying that.

"Her prince, huh?" The paramedic was paying more attention to checking the woman's blood pressure. But then she smiled at Lissa. "Glad to hear it. Every woman needs a prince, don't they?"

"I'd rather have a cat," Lissa said.

The paramedic laughed softly and waved at one of the other paramedics. "Bring the stretcher, Charlie."

The woman stirred slightly, but her eyes still didn't open. "It's okay, darlin'," Jed told her softly, encasing her hand in both of his. "You're gonna be fine now. You just relax."

"Are they taking her to the hospital?" Lissa asked.

"They have to," Jed told Lissa. "Holding her hand and talking to her isn't going to make her wake up."

"Daddy tried kissing her."

The paramedic laughed as she shoved her bag to one side. "We'll try a few other things first and if they don't work, we'll let your dad try kissing her again, okay?"

Charlie collapsed the legs of the stretcher so that it was on the floor next to the woman. "I think you'll have to let go now, sir."

"Oh, yeah. Sure."

They were moving the woman onto the stretcher and her hand came free from Jed's easily. As if she hadn't been clinging to him for all she was worth. Maybe he had imagined it. Just as he was imagining that her face went stiller and a touch paler as he stood up.

"You can come in the ambulance," the first paramedic told them. "Or you can follow us to the hospital. We're going to Memorial Hospital."

Go with? "No, no," he said. "I think you must have—"

But the paramedic was already moving away, the wheels of the stretcher crunching on the glass covering the floor. Someone gave him the woman's coat. Someone else handed him her purse.

"Wait, Daddy." Lissa had bent down to pick up her overnight bag and pulled a set of keys from under a nearby vending machine. "I think these are hers, too. Her name must be Karin. That's what it says on the key chain."

"Oh, yeah?" he said as Lissa handed him the keys. "We'll give these to the paramedics and they can make sure Karin gets them."

Lissa frowned, her eyes filled with puppy-dog sadness. "Can't we take them to her ourselves?" she asked. "Then we could make sure Karin's okay."

Part of him was tempted, but the stronger, smarter part knew better. "That would be butting in, Lissa," he said. "Karin's in good hands. She doesn't need us anymore."

Lissa trailed along after him toward the door. "The paramedic said every woman needs a prince."

"I'm not a prince," Jed pointed out. "I'm just an old rodeo cowboy."

He stopped in the doorway for Lissa so they could pick their way over the debris together. Broken glass, spilled trash, pieces of the glass and metal sign that had hung over the door. Everywhere they walked, there was a mess, though there was a narrow path that the paramedics had cleared for the stretcher.

Jed went over to the rear of the ambulance, waiting

a little ways off while they loaded the stretcher into it. The woman was lying still. Her face seemed even paler as a now-gentler rain kissed her skin.

Jed turned to look away, drawing in a deep, ragged breath. "Boy, that was some storm," he said to Lissa as he glanced around the parking lot. He would be glad once they were on their way again. This was a little unnerving, too much like roping a calf without the rope—suddenly he couldn't seem to do the simplest things.

"Daddy," Lissa said in a worried whisper.

He just shook his head. "It's okay, darlin'. She'll be fine. In fact—"

"No, Daddy, look over there," she said, pointing across the parking lot. Two trucks had pulled in. Two television-news trucks.

"Hey, look at that." It was the old man from inside. "Guess they're coming to take pictures of the hero here."

"You two are gonna be celebrities," the waitress said. She sounded as if she thought that prospect was exciting.

Jed's stomach fell about ten feet. He looked at Lissa and she stared back at him, her big brown eyes worried. Regretful. Resigned.

Damn. Double damn. "Where are your sunglasses?" he asked.

She shrugged and waved toward the restaurant. "In there someplace. I think I dropped them."

"Are you coming, sir?" the paramedic called. "We're ready to go."

Jed looked at the TV-news trucks with their satellite dishes and retractable antennae. Once they stopped, there would be no hiding. The story of the rescue would be told and then the reporters would come to interview him and Lissa. And they'd all recognize her. Her being here would be a big story, and once her face was on the news, they'd never be able to slip into the festival undetected. Her dream of reliving her mother's fun would never happen.

Lissa's only chance was if they left now. If they gave the coat and purse and car keys to the paramedic and raced for their car. It wasn't parked too far away, just over there—

Where the news trucks were stopping. Oh, hell. He wouldn't be able to move the car without asking them to move the trucks.

"Are you—" The paramedic stopped. "Oh, you've got your keys out. You going to follow us in your car?"

Jed looked at the keys in his hand. The keys had the Jeep Cherokee emblem stamped on them. And, parked not ten feet from him, was a Jeep Cherokee. He hit the keyless remote and the nearby car flashed its lights as it unlocked the doors.

Why not? Karin would need her car at the hospital anyway. And he and Lissa could get a ride back here later, after the news crews had gone.

"We'll pull up behind you," he told the paramedic.

Lissa grabbed the coat and purse from him. "I'm going to ride in the ambulance," she said.

"Lissa!" But she was already climbing in.

"That's fine," the paramedic said. "It'll help your wife relax to have your little girl with her."

"My what?" Jed stared at the woman as she climbed into the ambulance after Lissa. "But she's not—"

Off to his right, the doors of the news trucks opened. He saw the crew spilling out and heard a reporter ordering them about. It wasn't the time for arguments or discussions. Besides, the ambulance doors were shutting and the engine was running. He hurried over to the Jeep.

Within moments he was rolling out of the parking lot after the ambulance, the news trucks left behind. The paramedic's mistake was no big deal. He'd correct it once he got to the hospital.

Karin grimaced at the bright light shining in her face and tried to turn away. The darkness had been so warm and safe. It had left her feeling loved somehow, loved and cared for. She hadn't wanted to leave it.

"She's coming around," someone said.

But they weren't going to let her return to that safety, and the urge to retreat slipped slightly away. She squinted at the anxious faces around her. A couple of men, a woman and—Karin blinked—the cowboy and his daughter. Though the cowboy kept glancing out the curtains as if he was looking for someone—or bored. What was he doing here anyway?

"How many fingers am I holding up?" someone asked.

Karin turned to stare at him. It was a doctor. Then she remembered. Leaving the ladies' room at the tollway oasis. Arguing with the cowboy and a sound like a jet landing on the roof as all hell broke loose. She put her hand on her belly. Was her baby okay? It had to be. She had a headache but felt fine otherwise.

"Ma'am?" The doctor was holding up his hand in her face. "Can you tell me how many fingers I'm showing?"

"Three," the little girl answered.

"Lissa, honey," the cowboy corrected.

His voice did funny things to Karin's insides.

"I was just trying to help," the girl said.

Karin could hear the cowboy's boots shuffling on the floor. "Answering for the lady's not helping the doc see how bad she's hurt," he said.

The cowboy's voice was familiar somehow, in ways that felt warm and caressing. Maybe it was the soft drawl that was so easy on her ears. Or the way his low tones seemed to slide under her reserves and cuddle up to her. She wanted him to go on talking.

"What do you say we wait outside, Lissa?" he said. "See if we can find that paramedic."

Karin's spirits suddenly sagged. His talk about leaving didn't feel nearly as soothing to Karin's ears. It was dumb, she knew. And surely a sign that she'd been badly injured. She shouldn't care either way.

"No, you're fine here," the doctor was assuring him. "And Beverly's probably long gone."

Beverly? Karin's spirits took a nosedive, no longer sagging but now flattened on the ground. She took a deep breath, clamping down on her crazy reactions. It made no difference to her if he wanted to leave the cubicle to go talk to another woman. Who cared?

"I don't suppose it mattered anyway," the cowboy muttered with a resigned glance out the curtains' opening.

What doesn't? Karin wondered. Was he hoping to ask Beverly for a date?

The doctor was trying to claim Karin's attention. "Let's try again," he was saying to her. "And no prompting from the audience, please. How many fingers?"

Karin looked at the hand in front of her, suddenly all the more anxious to be out of here. "Two."

"Very good." He shone a light in her eyes, then stepped back to make a note in her chart. "How's your head? Aching?"

"It's fine. I'm fine," she said briskly. "When can I leave? I'm supposed to be at a wedding soon."

What time was it anyway? She looked around the cubicle. Emergency rooms always had clocks. Ah, there it was. And if she left now, she wouldn't be too late.

Swinging her feet to the side of the gurney, she sat up. Her head throbbed and the room swayed—but it wouldn't for long. If she just concentrated, she would be fine.

"Hey, wait a minute," the doctor said. "You aren't going anywhere yet. We need to get some test results back." He put his hand on her shoulder and pushed her gently down. "So you can just take it easy."

She didn't want to take it easy, but lying down did feel better. Though only for a minute. Once the room stopped spinning, she would catch her breath and sit up again.

"It looks like the lady here's doing good," the cowboy said. "So we'll just be on our way."

That was fine with Karin, but apparently not with the doctor. He closed her chart with a snap.

"Do you have to?" the doctor asked the cowboy. "I'd really rather someone stayed with her but I can't spare a nurse right now."

Karin didn't want or need anybody here. "I'm fine," she pointed out sharply. "You can all go."

"No, we can stay." The little girl had been staring out the slit in the curtains but turned around. "Can't we, Daddy? There's too many people outside the hospital right now anyway. It looks like somebody's there with a camera taking pictures.''

"Really?" The cowboy now sounded about as anxious to go out there as Karin was to go back to Chesterton this weekend.

But the doctor laughed. "The news crews always come here for footage after a big storm. You two must be the only ones in the area that don't want to be on the news.''

Not exactly. Karin had no desire to be on TV either. Though the Chesterton gossip network would be just as efficient.

"Guess we're private folks," the cowboy said. "Sure, we'd be glad to stay here a bit longer.''

But Karin had no desire to be cooped up with him...them. "I don't—"

The doctor pulled the curtains apart slightly. "I'll be back in a little while," he told the cowboy. "Call for the nurse if her condition seems to change." Then he left.

Karin waited a moment until the doctor's steps were lost amid the general noise of the emergency room, then she sat back up. The room only wobbled slightly.

"Hey, now, the doc didn't say you could get up," the cowboy scolded.

He was standing in the doorway as if he was waiting for the sheriff to arrive, his arms crossed over his chest, his hat in one hand. She glared his way. Her immunity to him was growing with each minute. His voice still seemed to glide over her skin like a caress, but that was just due to her injury. And if her insides felt particularly jellylike, it was due to her empty stomach, not his smile.

"I'm fine," she told him. "Feel free to look for

Beverly if you still want. I don't need anybody here with me.''

"Daddy doesn't need to talk to Beverly," the little girl said as she came closer. "I already did. Daddy just thinks he has to do everything."

She made the statement with such resigned weariness that Karin had to smile. "He does seem a little bossy," she agreed.

"Bossy?" he drawled. "I'm bossy just because I'm the only one here with any common sense?"

"See?" the girl said and sat down on the chair near the gurney. "I'm Lissa and that's my dad. His name is Jed."

Jed? Short and to the point. It fitted the man perfectly. Not that Karin was giving him any thought. "Lissa's a pretty name," she said.

"My real name's Melissa, but that's kind of dorky so I shortened it to Lissa. Karin's a pretty name, too."

"Thank you," Karin said even as she frowned slightly.

There was no reason to wonder how they knew her name. Her coat and purse were on the far chair. All they'd had to do was look in her wallet. And even if they looked all through her purse, they wouldn't know any more about her than her address and library-card number.

Yet she had this uneasy feeling that all her secrets had been exposed. That they knew everything about her—that she was the only girl in the sixth grade who didn't cry when they watched *Romeo and Juliet,* that she had her first date when she was a sophomore in college and then it was a blind date that ended before nine o'clock, and that she was scared to death about becoming a mother. She felt a wave of dizziness return.

''My father saved your life.''

Karin's eyes opened wide. ''He what?''

''Lissa.'' The frown on the cowboy's face deepened as he looked at Karin. ''I did no such thing, ma'am.''

There was a ruggedness about him. A toughness. Like you could lean on him, no matter how strong the storm. Too apt an analogy, Karin thought. She needed to get up off this gurney and leave.

''You did, too, Daddy.'' The girl turned toward Karin. ''It was his life force that pulled you through.''

''Life force?'' Karin said, her forehead wrinkling.

Lissa nodded. ''It flowed from his soul into yours.''

''I see.'' Though she didn't. Maybe it was one of those New Age things, something that wasn't covered in the *Journal of the American Medical Association*. And therefore something that ranked right up there with everlasting love and happily-ever-afters—all myths. Still, she didn't like to be rude.

She flashed her best professional smile at the cowboy. ''Well, thank you so much for your life force,'' she said. ''I appreciate it.''

''All I did was hold your hand,'' he said, his voice making it clear that this life-force stuff wasn't his idea.

Yet somehow his holding her hand seemed all the more dangerous. She glanced down at her hands, almost certain she could feel his touch even now. This was nuts. It was just the power of suggestion from her overactive brain. She had to get out of here and away from this cowboy. A little rest and she'd be as good as new.

''Well, thanks for holding my hand,'' she said and slipped off the gurney to her feet. ''I appreciate it, but—''

''Karin!'' Lissa cried.

Somehow Karin's knees had been replaced with rubber—soft, mushy rubber—and they wouldn't hold her up. She grabbed for the edge of the gurney but found Jed's shoulder instead. He was picking her up!

"You think now maybe you'll listen to the doc and take it easy?" he said. "Or am I being bossy again?"

She wanted to kick him, but it would take coordination she didn't have. So she just closed her eyes and lay her face against his chest for the brief endless moment that he held her before laying her back down on the gurney. His heart was beating so close to hers, and he smelled so good. She wanted—

"Karin? Karin Spencer?"

Karin turned, clutching Jed's shoulder instinctively as a smiling woman came bursting into the cubicle.

"Amy Dubonet," the woman said, advancing still farther into the cubicle. "From third-year French."

"Oh, right." Karin gave her uncertain smile several extra watts of certainty though she had no recollection of taking three years of French back in high school. "I'm sorry. How have you been?"

"Fine." Amy grinned and took a long slow look at Jed. "Although not as good as I hear you've been doing."

"What? Oh, my." Karin suddenly realized she was still in Jed's arms. Not only in his arms, but clutching as if the floor was covered with snakes. Her face burned with embarrassment and she slid from his arms to sit on the edge of the gurney. She felt a little weak and a little wobbly, but much more in control.

"You sure you're okay?" Jed asked.

Karin ignored him. Letting even his voice near her meant losing a piece of her control. And she had already lost too many pieces this afternoon. "So, Amy, what have you been up to? Do you work at the hospital?''

Amy laughed loudly. "Oh no you don't. You can't waltz into Memorial with this handsome hunk and then start talking about careers. We all want the juicy details. When's the wedding?''

"When's the what?" Karin had no idea what Amy was talking about.

"You must have misunderstood," Jed told Amy.

"Oh, I'm sorry. Was it a secret?"

"It's not anything," Jed said. "There's been a—"

"Hey, I gotta run," Amy said, giving Karin a quick wink. "I'll see you at Penny and Brad's wedding and you can tell all then."

"Wait a minute," Jed cried, then muttered something under his breath as Amy left.

Karin continued to stare at the space where Amy had been standing. She felt as if she'd been mugged. As if someone had snuck in and bopped her over the head. She wasn't even in town yet and the gossip network had struck. Somebody had seen Jed with her and the whole town had jumped to the conclusion that the two of them were a couple.

"Lissa, you stay here with Karin, will you?" Jed was saying. "I've got to go after that lady and clear this up."

As if it would be that easy. "It's just a silly misunderstanding," Karin said. She felt tired all of a sudden. This had been a hell of a day. "Somebody just jumped to conclusions like someone always—"

"I think it's more than that," he told her.

She stopped to stare at him. "More?" Maybe it was the bump to her head but she didn't understand.

He nodded. His eyes met hers but his earlier bravado

was gone. "The paramedic got the wrong idea. She thought we were married, but left before I could correct her. I tried to find her once I got to the hospital—"

"I told you I took care of it," Lissa cried. "I told her that you two weren't married."

Karin looked from Jed to Lissa and then back to Jed. A little flame of annoyance started to flicker but she tried to smother it. Maybe it was all a bad dream. Maybe she was still unconscious and imagining this.

She took a deep breath. "Now let me get this straight. This wasn't someone jumping to conclusions. This was someone actually saying to you that she thought we were married and you didn't correct her."

"There wasn't time," he said, sounding as if he was fighting his own impatience. "Now, I really ought to go—"

"There wasn't time? How much time does it take to say, 'No, you've got it wrong'?" she asked with a frown. The feeble control she had on her anger slipped a notch or two.

The whole scene played out in her mind like a bad horror movie—the paramedic told Amy and Amy told everyone on the hospital staff from Chesterton, and they all told their husbands and wives and sisters. By the time Karin got to Penny's wedding, the whole town would know. Worse, Karin's mother would know and be wiping away tears of joy. Once again, Karin would disappoint her mother and leave her to be the butt of jokes.

"There were other things going on at the time," Jed pointed out. "Like getting you to the hospital."

So there wasn't time for him to say three words— we're not married? Karin covered her face with her hands. "I can't believe you did this."

"It's not Daddy's fault," Lissa repeated, her voice wobbly. "I told the lady. She thought you were my mom and I said no, that you guys weren't married. That Daddy was just your prince."

Karin let her hand slip from her eyes. "My prince?"

The words came out a little more horrified than Karin intended and she clamped her mouth shut. So the town wouldn't think she was married, just deranged.

"That's what all the people at the restaurant said he was," Lissa said.

Karin forced a shaky laugh. This wasn't Lissa's doing. She couldn't let Lissa take on a share of his guilt. "Well, that's certainly something the town will enjoy—me having a prince."

Jed gave Karin a look, then thrust some money into Lissa's hands. "I saw some vending machines behind the nurses' station. Want to get us something to eat? Hunger's making us all a mite testy."

Lissa grasped the money and went toward the opening in the curtain. "Every woman needs a prince," she told Karin. "Everybody says so."

Karin smiled. "And now I've got one. Great." She would kill Jed, but not until Lissa was gone. She held her smile until the girl left and then a few moments longer to give Lissa time to move away from the cubicle.

Then she turned on Jed. "I can't believe you did this," she cried in a low whisper. "It's just perfect. It's all I needed to make my life complete."

But Jed didn't flinch back from her anger. "Well, I could clear it all up if you'd just let me go find this Amy."

"You just want to find Amy?" Karin snapped at him. He didn't get it. He didn't have a clue what was happening this very moment, even as they were stuck here arguing. "Talking to Amy won't do any good. She's told dozens of people by now. And they've each told dozens. By now, half the planet thinks we're a couple. They probably have us engaged."

He stared at her. "Why?"

She opened her mouth to continue her rant, then closed it again when no sounds came out. She tried again. "Why what?"

"Why would everybody be talking about this? Why would anybody care?"

His voice was so calm, so low and slow and soft with a drawl that teased at her anger, trying to defuse it.

"Back home, we talk about the things that surprise us. A calf being born with two tails. A bear that nursed a stray pup. Mrs. Hornway getting another tattoo. A beautiful woman having a beau wouldn't cause any talk at all. Unless, of course, your real beau is gonna get wind of this."

He was trying to trick her out of her irritation, but she wasn't going to get sidetracked. "I don't have a *real* beau," she pointed out. "But that's—"

"You don't have a beau?" He frowned at her. "What's the matter with men in the Midwest?"

"Why does there have to be something wrong with the men in the Midwest?" she snapped, looking him over from his booted feet to the cream-colored cowboy hat in his hand. His washed jeans snugly covered his— she looked away even as her heart began to race. She was not affected by his presence, not in the slightest.

"In the civilized world, it takes two equal partners to make a relationship," she said. "So if I'm not in one, it's my choice."

"The civilized world, huh?"

His voice was soft but she had a moment's misgiving. Maybe that had been the wrong way to put it. Maybe she should—

"I sometimes forget what life's like here in civilization," he said with an even slower drawl.

Karin felt her cheeks redden with heat. "I didn't mean anything by that," she assured him quickly. "Just that starting a relationship isn't like coming in and roping a cow. 'Oh, I like the way that one looks. I think I'll take it home.' Both parties have to be interested in the other for a relationship to happen."

"So you're saying I shouldn't be packing my lasso when I go to parties here in Chesterton, no matter how pretty the fillies are?"

For some unknown reason, Karin blushed. A full-body, head-to-toe, bright red blush. It was not caused by the idea of him going to parties in Chesterton. And certainly not by the idea of him being attracted to anyone here. Her reaction had to be the delayed effects of her injury.

"Make fun of me all you like," she said. "But you know what I mean."

He shook his head as he took slow steps closer to her. Her mouth went dry and her hands started to sweat. It wasn't that she was afraid of him—it was strange but she trusted him completely—but more that she was afraid of herself all of a sudden.

"You know," he said quietly. "You sure are a stubborn lady. I can see why plan B didn't work."

His eyes had hers locked in some sort of visual embrace that she could feel down to her toes, but she just lifted her chin slightly. Even if he did provoke some strange and unknown reactions in her, it didn't matter. She just wouldn't give in to them. "And just what was plan B?" she asked.

He smiled. "That I wake you up with a kiss."

Chapter Three

"This is ridiculous," Karin snapped. "It's totally unnecessary."

Jed drove through the intersection before he spoke. There wasn't much traffic, but he had a feeling he needed to be doubly careful here. Because things seemed so safe, it would be easy to let his guard down. Then something was sure to hit him.

"I'm sorry to argue with you, ma'am," he said a moment later. "But it's got to be done. I made the mistake, so it's my job to make it right."

"But not by coming to the wedding with me," she said. "It was a misunderstanding. I'll explain it all when I get there. Just drop me off and I'll get the car from your motel later. You don't need to do anything."

"I'm sorry, ma'am, but I do. A man doesn't let a lady take the blame for his mistakes."

Jed liked to think he was smarter than the average

calf and maybe even smarter than the average bull, but the way he'd handled things today seemed to put him on the level of the average rodeo barrel. Why the hell had he let his tongue get tangled in his feet when that paramedic had called Karin his wife?

He could feel the start of a headache of his own and no debris had hit him on the head. Maybe that life-force thing had actually been a trade—her aching head for his life force. He needed to clear up the misunderstanding and get him and Lissa on their way.

"Did you say to turn left at the next light, ma'am?" he asked Karin.

She was fixing her makeup, and didn't answer. Didn't even act as if she'd heard him.

"You know, 'ma'am' doesn't sound all that friendly," Lissa pointed out from the back seat. "Karin's going to think you don't like her."

Jed concentrated on his driving. He knew what Lissa was getting at, but he wasn't rising to the bait. Wendy had always told him that calling every woman darlin' was going to get him in trouble one day, and she'd been right. He'd only done it when Karin had been unconscious, but it still got him in trouble. And her along with him.

"It's okay," Karin said. "I don't care what your dad calls me as long as he lets me straighten out this mess. Yes, turn left up here."

Jed slowed down and turned. Karin's voice sounded tired, but then she'd been through a lot today. A concussion was bad enough without having to bear the burden of his stupidity.

"I'm going to get this all straightened out," he told her. "You don't have to do anything."

"Maybe I'd rather fix it myself," she told him. "The

last thing in the world I want is for you to get up in front of the wedding guests and announce we aren't engaged.''

"That's not exactly what I had planned," he said.

She checked herself out in the little mirror on the back of the car's sun visor, then flipped it back up with a dissatisfied snap. "Oh, what does it matter? This visit was doomed from the start."

It was thinking like that that worried him. Maybe it was just the concussion talking. She must have a fierce headache.

"I bet that's the place," Lissa said. "Lucky the storm missed here."

Off to their right was a gravel lane that led off through some trees, but at the head of the lane, on either side, the fence posts were decorated with a cascade of white flowers and balloons.

"Yep, that's Penny's tree farm," Karin said. "We used to love to come here and play as kids."

"Did you go barefoot?" Lissa asked.

"All summer."

"Did you climb trees and catch lightning bugs and eat homemade ice cream on the porch?"

Jed could feel Lissa latching on to Karin's memories. He knew Lissa needed this for some reason, but the whiteness of Karin's face worried him more at the moment.

"Lissa," Jed cautioned. "Karin's got a bad headache. Let her be."

"I'm fine," Karin protested. "And if I'm not, I'm certainly able to say so myself."

But she didn't look fine to him, no matter how much she insisted. She looked alone and afraid. He didn't say anything more though as he drove slowly down the lane—past a big, old-fashioned farmhouse, several barns and small groups of people walking toward some gardens. Everywhere he looked, there were garlands and cascades of flowers tied up with ribbons, yet it looked natural, as if the flowers all belonged there.

"Wow, this is sure pretty," Lissa said, her voice filled with wonder. "When I get married, I want it to look just like this."

"It does seem perfect, doesn't it?" Karin said, sounding strained.

Jed didn't say anything, not sure what to read in her voice. It wasn't jealousy certainly, but maybe loneliness. Maybe a sense of dreams that would never come true. Had she loved deeply and then been hurt? If so, he knew her pain, knew her certainty that love was a desert that you didn't wander anywhere near. You might find water and shelter, but it always dried up and left you worse off.

In silence, Jed pulled the Jeep into an empty parking spot. Lissa and Karin both got out before he could open their doors, and he had to satisfy himself with the gentlemanly chore of locking the car.

Karin had been starting across the yard, but turned with a frown at the sound of the key in the lock. "You don't have to do that here," she said. "No one's going to steal it."

"I figured that. I just didn't want to tempt an honest man into sin," he joked, wanting to see her frown go away.

"I resent that," she snapped. "These are my friends. No one is interested in that stupid car."

Locking a car was an insult now? He knew she wasn't feeling well, and obviously bothered by this whole wedding setting, but she could give him a break.

"Fine," he said. "If it bothers you, I'll leave the car open."

"You can do what you want. I don't care."

Ten years of marriage had taught him what that really meant. Jed just turned and hit the keyless entry. The doors unlocked with a little squawk. There. She'd won. She should be pleased now.

She wasn't.

"I said you could lock it." Karin came back, opened the passenger door, hit the powerlock and slammed the door closed. Then she turned toward him. "Now, are you happy?"

He looked at her, telling himself that she was injured, that she was possibly mourning a lost love, that she was having to explain a mistaken engagement to her friends and family. But she was also getting damn annoying.

"Bordering on ecstatic, ma'am," he murmured.

She spun around on her heel and started across the parking area. Lissa came over and took his hand as they followed.

"I think she likes you," Lissa whispered.

"I can see that," Jed said, swallowing a laugh. "She looks about ready to hug me to pieces."

"Karin, you're here!"

Two young women had been walking into the garden area but had turned and were now hurrying over to Karin. Another group must have heard their cries, since they were coming back also. And still others were hurrying across the parking area. Karin had stopped walking and was standing as still as a statue as a middle-aged woman hugged her tightly.

Jed forgot his annoyance and hurried over, pushing his way through the small crowd to Karin's side. "Excuse me, ma'am,'' he said. "Beg your pardon for interrupting but—''

The middle-aged woman had pulled away from Karin with a smile, but turned as Jed spoke. "Oh, Karin. A cowboy!'' she cried and threw her arms around him. "How absolutely, positively wonderful.''

Jed endured the hug for a moment, feeling guiltier and guiltier the longer he let it last. Finally he pulled away. The resemblance was strong, this had to be Karin's mother.

"Ah, Mrs. Spencer,'' he said. "It's a pleasure, ma'am.''

"Mrs. Spencer?'' The woman roared with laughter. "Honey, call me Marge. I haven't been Mrs. Spencer for more than thirty years. Just how long have you known Karin?''

Jed tried to keep smiling. This was the perfect opening. "Uh—''

But Marge gave him no chance. She spotted Lissa and enveloped her in a crushing hug. "Welcome to Chesterton, sweetie. I can't tell you how excited I am to meet you and your dad.''

Jed cleared his throat, then cleared it again when he saw Lissa returning the hug. Neither his parents nor Wendy's were still alive, but for a moment, Lissa had the grandmother she'd always wanted. Damn, this was getting complicated.

"Uh, ma'am,'' he said. "I'm afraid there's been a little misunderstanding here.''

Marge let go of Lissa to reach over and take Jed's hand. "Thank you from the bottom of my heart.'' The woman's eyes were glistening like those of someone whose prayers had been answered. "I've had nobody but Karin stick around all these years and now I'm going to have a real family.''

Jed swallowed quickly. "Actually, ma'am, it's not that simple."

She laughed with real glee and wagged her finger at him. "You don't have to confess," she said. "I know. I knew the moment I hugged her. You can't fool a mama.''

Jed was at a loss for words. He had a feeling Karin's mother wasn't talking about the same thing he was, but he pushed on. "It was all my fault, ma'am. I take all the blame.''

Her smile changed slightly. Not that it dimmed or anything, but it seemed to change from laughter to caring. "What a gentleman you are, but you know, I couldn't be happier." She leaned closer. "I never thought I'd have one grandchild and now to be getting two! It's too wonderful for words.''

Two grandchildren? Jed felt as if he'd been thrown and had landed on his head. Okay, Lissa was one grandchild Karin's mom thought she was getting, but where was the other one? Unless Karin had a child that she was keeping hidden—

Understanding came like a mule kick to his head and he turned to stare at Karin. He hadn't really looked before, hadn't really thought about her body, but that her dress was awfully baggy and not very flattering. Here in the gentle breeze, it flowed around her differently and he could see her swollen belly.

Oh, Lordy. The lady had a biscuit in the oven. She was a hundred percent pregnant. And all of Chesterton thought *he* was the daddy.

Karin slipped into the seat just as the music began to play. She hadn't exactly run from her mother and the other well-wishers, but she might have if the service hadn't been about to start. She just couldn't face everyone while Jed told them the truth.

There'd be pity in everyone's eyes, but no one would be surprised. They'd all think what fools they had been to have thought a man actually loved Karin, and that she had returned it. But her mother, the romantic, would publicly mourn the loss of Karin's love and then the laughter would start.

Feeling movement next to her, Karin turned. Her friend Dorothy had slipped into the seat next to her.

"Dorothy!" Karin cried in a whisper, enveloping the woman in a hug. "I thought you were in Paris."

"Nope, I just got in. I wouldn't miss this for the world. I'm not sure I'm ready to forgive Heather for cheating us out of a wedding by eloping."

Karin was still stunned at the speed of her other friend's wedding but just smiled. "Didn't she always say she was going to elope?"

Dorothy nodded. "Yeah, but you said a team of horses would have to drag you to your wedding. We never took either of you seriously."

Luckily the procession had started and Karin didn't have to respond. She didn't have to say that had been a joke or that this whole engagement was a misunderstanding or that she was never ever getting married.

Heather, Penny's matron of honor, came down the aisle first. She looked wonderful in a pale pink dress, but even more remarkable was the glow in her cheeks and the gleam in her eye.

Karin leaned over closer to Dorothy. "How did Penny ever convince timid little Heather to be her matron of honor?"

"Because timid little Heather isn't nearly so timid anymore," Dorothy whispered back. "She's really different since she fell in love. I've talked to her a few times and can't believe the change in her."

Karin watched as Heather reached the arbor where the minister waited. Heather's husband, Alex, was the best man and his eyes glowed with such love for her that it almost took Karin's breath away. Could love really be so strong that it could change who you were?

But then Penny was starting up the aisle, looking absolutely beautiful. Flowers were woven through her golden-blond hair and her white gown was flowing like a soft cloud around her. But when she joined Brad at the arbor, all you could see was the radiance of her love for him.

Karin settled back in her chair, listening to the ceremony but also fighting off a heaviness in her own heart. The feeling was probably just due to the bump on her head—because she was really and truly happy for her friends—but she also felt sad. She had come to terms long ago with the fact that she could not love, so this just had to be the lingering effects of a concussion. Or worry over having to handle the pity party that would be held for poor not-engaged Karin once the ceremony was over.

So she forced herself to concentrate on the sweet scent of flowers in the air, on the warm sunshine and the fact that she was here with her friends. She was a wee bit sorry she let Jed and Lissa take her car. It would have been nice to have a way to escape if things really got bad.

All too soon the minister was pronouncing Penny and Brad husband and wife, and the bride and groom had kissed and were walking back down the aisle. Time to face her mother's disappointment. She got to her feet.

"Wasn't that the most perfect wedding ever?" Dorothy asked as they made their way slowly toward the receiving line at the other side of the garden. She dabbed at her eyes and sniffed. "I can't believe that two of us are married all of a sudden and I hear you'll be next. When's the big day?"

Karin swallowed hard. If Dorothy had just arrived, how had she heard that piece of news but not the correction? Karin would have thought it would be what everyone was talking about. "Actually, it's all been a crazy mixup," she said slowly.

"Oh?" Dorothy stared at her.

Karin took a deep breath. "It's really pretty funny. You see—"

"There you are." The deep drawling voice came from behind Karin and she spun around. There stood Jed, in jeans and a cowboy hat but still looking as if he belonged. There was a soft smile on his face. "You ran off so fast I was worried we lost you."

What was he still doing here?

"Is this him?" Dorothy stuck her hand out. "I'm Dorothy Williamson. I'm the one that kept Karin from killing Ted Michaels in first grade."

Karin blanched slightly at the reference. Like Jed would care, even if he knew the story.

Jed took her hand with a smile. "Jed McCarron at your service, ma'am. And I'm certainly glad you were there to stop the murder. I might never have met Karin if she'd been in jail."

Dorothy squealed with delight. "Oh, Karin, you are so lucky."

Karin took a deep breath. "Actually—"

"Actually, I need to steal Karin away for a minute," Jed said quickly as he took her arm. "Hope you'll excuse us, ma'am."

"Only if you promise to tell me later how you two met," Dorothy said.

"That'll make a great story," Karin said under her breath, but Jed was already leading her away. Her hand in his felt all too comfortable so she snatched it back. "What do you want? I was just about to tell Dorothy it was all a misunderstanding. She somehow got the first story but not your correction."

Jed's brown eyes were scolding. Even when he smiled and nodded at someone passing behind her, his eyes never lost that slightly angry look. "I haven't quite got to the correction yet," he admitted in a low voice.

"Why not?" she said. "That was the whole reason you came here."

"It was. But it seems you forgot to warn me of all the complications."

Was he trying to weasel out of telling the truth? It wasn't as though she'd asked him to. "What complications? I told you what the town was like when it came to gossip."

"You didn't tell me you were pregnant," he whispered.

Karin had had her mouth open to continue the argument, but nothing came out. She'd lost all power of speech. A couple of quick breaths later, she tried again.

"How'd you find out?" she asked.

"Your mother told me."

"My mother? But I haven't told her yet."

He looked down at her belly with a frown. "After a

while, some things don't need telling. What are you? Five months?"

She lifted her chin a touch, just to keep from looking too pitiful. "I don't see how that's any business of yours."

"Since your mother presumes I'm the father, it is," he snapped.

"Well, we can easily dispel that presumption, can't we?" she snapped back. What was he—afraid she was going to try to pin something on him? What a joke. She wasn't even trying to pin anything on the real father.

"We can't dispel anything here," he said, his voice back to being low. He smiled again at someone passing behind her, but his gaze was frosty when it returned to her. "Your mother's riding in the clouds. If we tell her now, she's got no place to go to deal with her disappointment."

Once again, he took her by surprise. So much so that she stared at him for a long moment. "You mean, you'll go on with the pretense just to save my mother's feelings?" she asked.

"She's a fine lady and doesn't deserve that load of hurt in public."

Damn. A rock'em, sock'em, rough, tough cowboy with a heart. That was like a horse that could fly. It didn't compute.

But Karin's eyes were misting up and all she could do was look away. "Thank you," she murmured.

She wished for a split second that they could keep up the pretense. Not for ages, but just long enough so that her mother could tell everyone Karin had changed her mind, not that the whole engagement had been a misunderstanding.

* * *

Dorothy couldn't help turning back around to watch Karin and Jed as she walked toward the receiving line. It was great to see Karin with someone, though it was a bit of a surprise. Maybe it was to Karin, too, since she seemed so flustered.

"Dorothy Williamson," someone behind her cried. "Land sakes, young lady, I thought you were in Paris."

Dorothy turned to find old Mrs. Jamison there. She gave her former fourth-grade teacher a big hug. "I was in Paris," Dorothy said, "but I had to come back for the wedding. It's not every day that one of my best friends gets married."

"But it's not every day that one of my former students does something as exciting as moving to Paris." The old woman hugged her back but then kept a hold of Dorothy's hand even as they pulled apart. "If I was twenty years younger, I'd have dumped Hank and come with you."

Dorothy smiled. Actually, her life in Paris wasn't all that exciting. An apartment and a job. Some good food. But nobody to talk to, nobody to laugh with. Nobody to confess to that working as a real estate agent in Chesterton hadn't been all that bad. Nobody like Toto, who had gone from boyfriend to friend but was still the only person she could really really talk to.

"Dorothy, is that really you?" It was Mrs. Brewster from the bakery enveloping her in a mammoth hug. "My stars, you look wonderful! Paris must agree with you."

"Can you say something in French?" one of Mrs. Brewster's daughters asked.

"Have you been to the top of the Eiffel Tower?" another one asked.

"Oh, can you come to my French class on Monday and tell us all about France?" someone else asked.

"I've only been in Paris so far," Dorothy felt bound to point out.

"You know," Mrs. Jamison said with a laugh, "they had to add two more sections of French I at the junior high. After you left, all the seventh-grade girls wanted to take French."

"Heavens." Dorothy wasn't sure what to say. She hadn't thought anyone noticed she was going.

"My mom says your leaving town was the best thing ever," some other young girl announced.

Before Dorothy could feel more than mildly stunned, all the other girls were nodding solemnly. "You showed us that we don't have to hang around Chesterton and get married after high school."

"That there's all sorts of things we can do instead."

"We all want to be just like you."

Mrs. Jamison gave her hand a final squeeze, then let go. "It's not everyone who has so many people looking up to her."

"Or who makes such an impact just by leaving town," Dorothy added.

Everyone laughed, and no one seemed to notice that she wasn't exactly laughing with them.

"Dorothy?"

Her heart seemed to stand still. She turned ever so slowly. Toto was at her side. She smiled at him, a weak imitation of the earth-shattering feelings washing over her. It seemed years since she'd seen him, not just a few weeks.

"Hi," she said. "How are you?"

He shrugged. "Same old, same old. Don't have to ask how you are, though. I can see Paris agrees with you."

"It sure does," one of the girls agreed. "It's exciting."

"It's wonderful," another said.

"It's magical," a third added.

Dorothy looked at the eager faces around her and then at Toto. She couldn't read anything in his eyes. She used to be able to. Maybe she had been gone longer than she thought. In any case, she could not— would not—express any doubts about her move. She'd made her bed, now it was time to lie in it. Even if that meant lying there alone.

Jed was not happy. It wasn't because he was at a wedding reception with a couple hundred people he didn't know. Or because he was supposedly engaged to a stranger. It was because they should have left an hour ago. Karin looked tired, her voice had long ago lost its smile and her step was dragging.

For some reason, he was feeling more and more responsible for Karin. He'd be glad once he was done steering her through this reception and able to admit the truth.

"You look downright awful, ma'am," he told her as they finally broke away from a group of her grade-school acquaintances that had stuck tighter than burrs to a dog's tail. "You ought to be home resting."

She frowned at him. "Does that smooth talking work on cows?" she asked. "It doesn't do much for me."

"You're pale," he pointed out.

"I'm always pale. I have pale skin." She smiled and

murmured a greeting to a couple passing by. ''I feel fine.''

He should just take her at her word. She was an adult, after all, and only a pretend fiancée. But there was something so vulnerable about her. A timid young girl trying so hard to be brave. Which was about as nuts as it got. She had to be the most pigheaded woman he'd ever met.

''Want to take a walk?'' she asked him suddenly.

''Over to the car? I'd be delighted, ma'am.''

Her lips tightened into an impatient line. ''I'm fine,'' she said. ''I just wanted to talk.''

Jed offered Karin his arm and let her lead him down a deserted-looking garden path. He might have made a joke about being led down the primrose path if he wasn't sensing how tired she was.

''How about we take a walk, then get some food and go?'' he said. ''You've had a rough day.''

She stared at him for a long moment, then laughed quietly. ''How about a rough few months?'' She leaned slightly into him.

It was only natural to put his arm around her shoulders. She needed his support, needed his strength. That was all it was—on both their parts.

They walked in silence amid beds of wildly blooming flowers, meeting fewer and fewer people as they strolled away from the reception garden. Jed was amazed at the different kinds of flowers everywhere and at the number of blooms.

''How'd she get everything to bloom for the wedding?''

''Oh, knowing Penny, she simply asked the flowers to wait to bloom until her wedding day.'' They arrived at a stone bench under an old oak tree and Karin sat down with a sigh, then looked around at the garden. "It is pretty amazing, isn't it? It's almost as if the plants all knew how much she loves Brad and conspired to make this a perfect day."

Jed looked at Karin. The garden was sure pretty, but there was something in her voice that drew him. A wistfulness. A sense of something that would never be.

Whatever mood was on her, she seemed to shake it off and turned to him. Her eyes weren't windows into any part of her. She was all business.

"I've been thinking about this engagement nonsense," she said slowly. "It really is a mess, isn't it?"

"Maybe I was wrong to wait," he said. "Maybe it would have been best to tell your mother right away. But she seemed so happy and I thought it would..."

She took his hand in hers. It surprised him, given her businesslike manner. It also seemed to warm something deep inside him that he wasn't going to think about.

"I don't want my mother hurt," Karin told him. "And I don't want her laughed at."

"Who'd laugh at her?"

Karin shrugged and looked down at their hands, still entwined. "My mother owns a bar—a cowboy bar. It's called The Corral, and romantic that she is, she keeps thinking every jerk who walks through the door is the cowboy who's going to ride off with her into the sunset. So she keeps falling in love—but with real losers. They make a fool of her and everyone snickers behind her back."

Jed shook his head. "Most of the people I met here seem to like her."

"My father ran off when I was three," she said and looked away. "Then, when I was in first grade, Ted

Michaels told the whole class my stepfather had gone to a motel with his older sister.''

He winced at the pain in her voice. ''The almost-murder,'' he said with a nod of comprehension.

Karin went on. ''When I was in fourth grade, my mother had to bail a different stepfather out of jail for writing bad checks, which she tried to make good on since they were mostly to people in town. Then he skipped bail and we lost our house.''

''But she had nothing to be ashamed of,'' Jed pointed out.

''When I was in eighth grade, I had yet another stepfather. This one couldn't hold down a job to save his life, yet he sure had expensive tastes. Fancy cars, nice clothes. She ran herself into the ground trying to please him and he still left—with the car and clothes she bought him. She was still paying them off years later.''

''So she's not the best judge of men—''

''All of her humiliations have been public ones,'' Karin said. ''I can't let her face another one.''

''I can see that.'' He suspected that Karin had tried to protect her mother's honor each and every time another husband vanished, too. ''There's no big rush. Once I take you to her place tonight, we can—''

Karin dropped his hand and began to wipe at a non-existent spot on her skirt. ''I'm not sure that would be a good time either.''

''Not tonight?'' Maybe he was misunderstanding. ''When do you think I should tell her?''

She glanced up at him, a hasty, lightning-quick glance that left him with the impression of pain and fear and worry and bravery. ''Maybe when we're both gone.''

Damn. That mule had kicked him in the head again.

"I'm sorry, ma'am," he said carefully. "I'm not following you."

She turned to face him then, her jaw set with something he was coming to recognize as stubbornness. "It's simple," she said. Her words tumbled out in a rush. "We're both leaving as soon as the Oz festival ends. Why not pretend we're engaged for the next week? Once we're gone, I'll say we broke the engagement."

"But wouldn't that just be making matters worse?"

"People break engagements all the time. And this way, she could tell people in her own time."

Jed just looked at her, into her blue eyes that he realized suddenly weren't the color of an icy lake, but of the early-morning sky when the world was soft and vulnerable. He sighed, something twisting around inside him.

"This is insane, ma'am," Jed told her. "What about the father of your baby? What if he should come around?"

Clouds came into that new morning sky and blotted away the hope. "His lawyer assured me he won't."

Jed felt the bite of anger. "Calling him a swine or a snake doesn't seem fair to the animal," he said.

She laughed. It was the first real laugh he'd heard from her, and it startled him. Brought a real smile to his lips, too, and suddenly he found himself staring at her mouth and wondering what it would be like to kiss her. Staring at her hair and wondering what it would feel like to run his fingers through. Staring at her—

He jerked back on his reins and held himself steady. It was just a momentary slip, nothing he had to worry about. "Still, living a lie doesn't seem right. I think I should tell your mother the truth this evening and have it over and done with.''

She said nothing for a long moment. ''What if I could promise you Glinda? That's why Lissa wanted to come, right? She wants to talk to Glinda. Well, if you help me, I'll help you make Lissa's wish come true.''

For a moment, he was ready to agree, but then sanity reclaimed him. ''There's no real Glinda,'' he said.

''You've never been to the festival before, have you?'' she said. ''For three days, Oz comes to life. So yes, there will be a Glinda. I know because this year it's me.''

''You?'' Jed sank back with a sigh.

''I'm one of the grand marshals of the festival,'' she explained. ''Each year the grand marshals are given a character from the story to portray. I was given Glinda. So throughout the festival, I *am* Glinda, puffy dress, wand and all.''

''Oh.'' So she really would be able to grant Lissa's wishes and maybe answer the mysterious question.

If he agreed to this pretend engagement.

One week and one little white lie really wasn't asking much, he told himself, not in return for Lissa's healing. It wasn't such a hard way to help Karin either. And the mix-up was his fault. As a gentleman he should be willing to agree to her crazy plan, regardless of what he'd get out of it. So why was he hesitating?

He had no idea. It had something to do with the blue of her eyes and the occasional quiver in her voice. With the tingle his lips still felt from that kiss he'd given her hours ago. It had everything to do with staying safe.

But he'd only be in danger if he let himself. All he had to do was keep his reactions under control. He just had to be careful. But hell, it would be no different than riding a bull—keep your wits about you and hold on tight.

He looked over at her. "If you'll have me as your intended for the next week, I'd be honored, ma'am."

She got to her feet, relief making her look weary again. "I think maybe you shouldn't keep calling me ma'am then," she noted.

"Only if I can take you home now."

She nodded and let him take her hand. They walked in silence back to the reception, though a million questions were running through his head. They ought to be planning things out and comparing stories, but she seemed too tired for that now. And he wasn't going to push her.

Once back in the reception crowd, they saw her mother and Lissa at a table by the garden's edge. Marge frowned as Karin and Jed approached and he knew that she saw how tired Karin looked. She said something to Lissa and they both came over.

"Karin's had a long day, ma'am," he told her. "I'll just take her on to your place then Lissa and I'll head on out."

"Out where?" Marge asked.

"Uh…" Damn, in this for barely a minute and he was slipping off the bull already. "We didn't want to crowd you, so I reserved a motel room for me and Lissa."

"That's silly," Karin's mother cried. "I know I've just got an apartment, but it's got enough room."

"Yeah," Lissa agreed. "Me and Grandma already figured it out."

Grandma? Jed frowned. Lissa knew this was pre-

tense, didn't she? She'd been there for the misunder-
standings and discussions. "What did you figure out?"

"That I'll sleep in Grandma's room with her."

"And...?" He was almost afraid to ask.

"And you can sleep with Karin in her old bedroom," Lissa said with a decisive nod. "Isn't that
neat?"

Jed stared at his daughter, his stomach slowly curling
into a ball. This was not the way to keep his reactions
in control. "*Neat* ain't the word for it, honey," he said
slowly.

Chapter Four

A night had never been so long. From his spot on the trundle bed on the floor, Jed watched the minutes drag by on Karin's digital clock. Every once in a while a car would drive by and the reflected lights would splash against the drapes and then fade away. Eight cars passed the first hour, the number dwindling with each hour. He'd heard a dog barking around three, but nothing since.

No, that wasn't quite accurate. He'd heard Karin's soft breathing all night long, as well as an indistinct murmur every so often. He'd sensed her restlessness when she'd stirred on the bed slightly above his and off to the side. And he'd breathed in the faint scent of her cologne and her childhood memories which filled the room.

This was all a gigantic mistake. He would have to

tell her their ruse wasn't going to work. As for Lissa and Glinda, well, he'd take his chances.

Finally the sun started to ooze through the beige drapes, giving the room a golden glow. With light, the hulking shapes on the shelves became teddy bears and the dark shadows revealed themselves as books. *Nancy Drew's Secret of the Old Clock. Cherry Ames, Student Nurse. Mr. Wizard's Book of Science.*

He glanced up at the bed where Karin lay. One arm near the edge was about all that he could see. What did those books say about her? Did she see herself as a detective, a nurse or a scientist? What was she now anyway? He was beginning to realize he knew nothing about her. How had he ever thought they could carry off this pretense for a week?

Then she stirred and moved her bare leg near the edge of the bed. Trim and shapely, a woman's leg with all the inviting curves that set a man's belly on fire. He rolled over on his side to look away.

This was pure insanity. He definitely had to cancel this agreement. He and Lissa had a great vacation planned. They didn't need to add anything or anyone to make it more complete.

Even though he was looking away, he could feel Karin behind him. Still sense the rhythm of her breathing, feel the inviting warmth of her skin.

Lordy, he was feeling like some moonstruck junior-high kid. Suffering from a mad crush on—

"Are you awake?" she asked.

Jed's heart stopped. Panic swept over him. Had she somehow overheard his thoughts? He sat straight up— and rammed his shoulder into the overhang of her old desk.

"Damn it," he muttered, holding his shoulder. "Damn it all to hell."

"Are you okay?"

He could hear her moving across her bed toward him. Was she going to climb down into his bed? That was the last thing he wanted.

"I'm fine. I'm fine," he said and scooted to the far side of his bed.

"Are you sure? It sounded like you whacked yourself awfully hard."

"Hey, I'm tough. Takes more than a little bump to hurt me."

She stopped moving. He could sense her pulling back. "I told you not to put your bed so close to my desk," she said.

Better than close to her bed. "I didn't want to be in your way."

"I'm not that clumsy." She sighed and settled back on her bed. "At least not yet."

Jed didn't say anything as he lay back down on the bed. Wendy had been at her most beautiful when she'd been pregnant with Lissa. There had been a glow about her, a sensuous richness that had drawn him to her. Karin didn't seem to be as comfortable in her pregnancy, at least not yet, but she had that glow that made her a feast for his eyes. Another reason why he had to tell Karin he'd changed his mind.

"So how'd you sleep?" Karin asked.

"Uh, fine," Jed said, trying to slow his racing heart. "And you? How's the head this morning?"

"Fine. Only a little ache." There was a long moment of silence. "I just wondered if it would bother you, sleeping in here with me."

Not unless counting her every breath was a bother.

"No, no. It was fine." Heavens, couldn't he think of another word? "Don't see that we had much choice."

"I suppose you could have insisted on going to a motel."

He wasn't sure what that little undercurrent in her voice meant. "Is that what you would have rathered?"

"Me?" she answered quickly. "Oh, no, this was no problem."

They lay there in silence for a long moment. He was carefully studying the ceiling, looking for advice in the bumpy plaster surface. Just how was he supposed to tell her he'd changed his mind?

"You know, I really appreciate your doing this," she said. "You probably think it's pretty pitiful that I even asked, but I couldn't face everyone alone. Not after the rumor got started."

By him. He felt like a calf being let out of the chute, a team of ropers right on his tail.

She went on. "It's just that all my life it seemed like someone was laughing at me or my mother and I couldn't take it anymore."

The lead man had the rope around his neck. "It's okay," he muttered.

"And it's not like I have anyone to blame but myself for being pregnant," she said. "I never thought Rico loved me. Well, not really. Not when I thought about it logically."

The back man got his legs and Jed was caught. "Really, it'll be fine," he said. "It's no big deal."

"If you don't want to go through with this, I'll still be Glinda for Lissa," she said. "I wouldn't disappoint her."

He wanted to groan. He wanted to cry out in agony,

but he swallowed his chance to escape. "No. We'll play this out as we planned."

"Well, I don't want you to feel that you can't have your vacation or do what you had planned."

Was she firing him or just giving him a long leash? "I probably shouldn't pick up too many ladies at the local bar though."

She rolled over on her side to look down at him. "Was that what you wanted to do?"

She sounded so serious, so worried, that he had to smile. "No, ma'am. I was only pulling your leg."

For some reason, they both looked at her leg. The covers had fallen back and it was exposed. The ankle had such a sweet curve to it that climbed up over the calf and then slid past the knee to—

She pulled the sheet over her leg and lay back again, but not before he saw her face turn a delicate shade of pink. This was not doing much to slow his racing heart.

He cleared his throat and went back to his contemplation of the ceiling. "I didn't have a whole lot planned actually," he said. "We need to get our car from the tollway oasis. It's got our luggage in it and we're not going to last long with the stuff in Lissa's bag."

"We can drive over there today. It's not too far, so once we do that, you and Lissa will still have almost the whole day free."

"Great." But what about her? No, that was dumb. This was her home. She'd have all sorts of people and places to visit. He didn't have to worry about her.

"I have no idea what Lissa will want to do." He made his voice brisk. "She's got a list a mile long of vacation activities."

"Oh?"

Was it his imagination or did she sound wistful? "You're more than welcome to join us if you'd like."

"Thanks, but I don't think so." She paused. "Well, maybe sometimes just so nobody gets too suspicious."

"No, we wouldn't want that."

"I have festival events to attend though, so nobody should think anything of us going our separate ways."

"Should work out well then."

"Yeah. We may hardly see each other."

That was probably for the best.

"Except here at night, of course," she added.

"Right. Except at night." And even that wouldn't be a problem anymore. He wouldn't let it be.

Suddenly there was a knock at the door and it opened slightly. Marge poked her head in. "You two had better get yourselves dressed. It's almost time to go."

"Go?" Jed asked.

Marge shook her head. "To church. Land sakes, cowboy. The town is dying to meet you. It's not every day Karin brings home a man. You two aren't going to have a minute to yourselves for the next week."

It wasn't exactly what Karin had envisioned but it would please her mother. And everyone in town—well, at least the churchgoing folks of Chesterton. They would make this public appearance at church and then everyone would forget about them. She just had to play the part of a fiancée for a few hours and then she could go back to worrying about impending motherhood.

"Park over there," her mother instructed from the back seat.

"There are closer spaces," Karin pointed out as Jed was pulling into the spot.

''Oh, leave those for the old folks that have trouble walking.'' Marge leaned forward over the seat back and put her hand on Karin's shoulder. ''Walking doesn't bother you, does it, honey? I never thought about that.''

''No. I'm fine.''

''Are you sure?'' Jed asked.

There was a look in his eye that annoyed her for some reason. She never should have confessed so much of her personal life this morning, about being laughed at as a child and her foolishness with Rico. Jed was going to feel as though he should hover over her.

Now he was feeling sorry for her and that was ten times worse than being laughed at. Why hadn't she kept her mouth shut?

''I'm fine,'' she repeated. ''I have no trouble walking. I like to walk.''

''Great.'' Her mother sank back onto her own seat. ''This will give everybody waiting outside church a good long look at my new family.''

Karin could have groaned aloud. Why hadn't she thought about that?

Jed had seen her mother's motives and had tried to warn her, but she had stupidly read his gaze wrong. Of course, he could have just said something. What was his thing with meaningful looks? How was she supposed to know what he was thinking? This really was all his fault.

''Heavens, Mother,'' Karin said with a sly smile aimed at Jed. ''You're going to embarrass Jed. He's actually rather shy.''

Jed smiled back as he turned off the engine. ''Nonsense, sweetheart,'' he said ever so lovingly. ''Besides, when I'm with you, I know no one's looking at me anyway.''

His words caught Karin off guard and she felt her cheeks burn. If he thought that she...

Karin took a deep breath. What was she thinking? One word from Jed and this whole facade was over. And much worse than having a broken engagement would be everyone finding out she was only *pretending* to be engaged. Her mother would never live that one down.

''That's so sweet of you,'' Karin murmured, the words painful to get out nonetheless. ''But I was just kidding. I don't think there's a shy bone in your body.''

''How can a bone be shy?'' Lissa asked.

Marge laughed and opened her door. ''Come on, Lissa. Let's you and me get going and leave these love-birds to peck and coo all they want.''

''What's pecking and cooing?'' Lissa asked as she got out after Marge.

Karin couldn't hear her mother's response, but didn't need to. She took a deep breath. ''Guess it's time to face the firing squad,'' she said and opened her door.

''Don't move,'' Jed snapped as he jumped out of the driver's side.

Don't move? Why not? What in the world was the matter?

Then Jed was around to her side, his hand held out to her. She put her hand in his—an annoyingly pleasant place for it to be—and got out of the car, looking around cautiously.

''What was that all about?'' She tried to peer around Jed, but he was blocking her line of vision.

''A gentleman helps a lady out of a car,'' he said as

he put her hand on his arm. "Opens her door, too, if she'd give him a chance."

"That was it? You made me think I was about to be attacked by a swarm of killer bees so you could help me out of the car?"

He leaned in close, so close that it almost felt as if his lips were touching her cheek. Or was it just his breath? Why was her heart racing so?

"We're in the show ring, remember," he warned.

She glared at him, at his typical cowboy attire of blue jeans, cotton shirt, boots and hat. His predictability was just as annoying as he was. Always looking right, sounding right, being right.

"Don't you ever wear anything other than that?"

"No, ma'am," he said and slightly pushed his hat back on his head. "I don't have much choice since we don't have our luggage yet, but even if I had all my clothes here, I'd still be wearing these clothes. A cowboy's not a cowboy without his hat and boots, and blue jeans are God's most perfect clothes, so it would feel like a sin to wear something else."

She really wanted to argue with him, but on him, they were the perfect clothes. And this wasn't the time or place for a scene. She smoothed her frown into a smile, glanced over toward the church and forgot her annoyance with him.

It looked as if half the town was out front, watching them. And every one of the people there had a sappy smile on their face.

"I feel a bout of morning sickness coming on," she told him.

He slipped his arm around her shoulders, and for a split second she leaned into his strength. Even more frighteningly, she almost wished she had the right to lean into it.

"Morning sickness won't work. That's a first trimester thing."

"Maybe I'm doing things in a different order." She straightened up and they started walking toward the church.

"Well, maybe not the preferred order, but I think there are some things that you can't really control."

"What do you mean the preferred order?"

"You know, have a father ready to help raise the kid."

Her steps faltered. She felt as if he'd hit her, and for some reason it hurt far more than it should have. "There are lots of single mothers bringing up fine children."

"That doesn't mean it's the preferred way to raise a child."

"Depends on what the father prefers, doesn't it?"

"I guess. But I was talking about ideals."

"A perfect world." She managed a smile for those watching, though her insides ached. "I don't know about you, but I don't live there."

"Guess if either of us did, we wouldn't be here now, would we?"

There was such a wealth of sadness in his voice, such infinite loneliness that her annoyance seemed petty. She tightened her hold on his arm, pulling him closer at the same time. The crowd was waiting.

"A few minutes now and a few minutes after the service," she said. "Then we can have a breather for the rest of the day."

"That's assuming we don't drown in good wishes first," he said.

They didn't exactly drown, but Karin did feel swamped. Old friends, old acquaintances, people who looked only barely familiar surrounded them, shaking Jed's hand, hugging Lissa until her hat seemed permanently askew, and kissing Karin on the cheek.

"Karin, how good to see you."

"What a handsome young man."

"And a ready-made family."

"How did you meet?"

"What does he do?"

"Do we see booties in your near future, not just wedding bells?"

"Later all," Marge called, Lissa firmly in hand as she led them into the church.

Karin followed along but felt all quivery inside. So much for loose-fitting dresses. And Jed was right. Babies needed fathers, too. Her baby especially. What kind of mother was she going to be if she couldn't even love—if she had no heart?

She glanced at Jed as they settled into a pew near the front. He was straightening Lissa's bonnet, pulling it down lower over her face. She was frowning but it was obvious that she cared about her father and respected him. Karin could tell he was a good father. Was there any chance that she could talk him into keeping up the pretense a little longer—like maybe another twenty years?

By the time the service ended, Karin was exhausted and ready to spend a quiet day at home. Except that her mother had other plans.

"We have to go to brunch at the Landing," Marge said once they'd braved the gauntlet of good wishes on their way out of church. "The Ingersolls invited us and I accepted. We can't not show up."

Brunch at the Landing, the most popular restaurant in town. Karin used to consider eating there a treat, but today it would be torture. Every churchgoer in Chesterton would be there.

"But maybe we had other plans," Karin said.

"Did you?" Her mother sounded surprised at the idea.

"No, it's fine," Jed said as he got them all into the Jeep. "Karin's appetite's been uncertain lately, that's all. There're some foods that she can't bear to even see."

"Really?" Lissa said. "I can't stand to look at mushrooms."

Karin smiled at the girl. "I can't stand them, either."

"Mushrooms taste great and they're nutritious," Jed said.

"They're fungi," Karin pointed out. "Yucky-tasting fungi, at that."

"You only think that because you've never had fresh ones cooked the McCarron way," Jed said.

Karin made a face at him. "Oh, right. Like that's—"

"Why haven't you had them?" Marge asked.

Karin caught herself at the same moment Jed did. For a moment there, they'd forgotten. No, she'd forgotten. Jed's face looked the same. No sudden flush of guilt. No worried look that he'd let something slip he shouldn't have. She was the one that had to be more careful.

"It's an ongoing argument we've been having," Jed told Marge. "I keep wanting to cook her up some mushrooms and she keeps refusing."

"Karin, Karin," her mother scolded with a laugh. "How many times do I have to tell you to be more adventurous? Try new things."

Karin contented herself with giving Jed directions to the restaurant. Try new things? Hadn't she been doing that when she went out with Rico? And wasn't this whole engagement nonsense something new? No, it was trying new things that was getting her in trouble. She liked the old ways, the safe ways. The ways she knew inside and outside.

Jed parked the car and they went into the restaurant. They found themselves surrounded by a new group of townsfolk, only this time they didn't have the excuse of a church service to help them escape.

"So how'd you two meet?" someone stopped by their table to ask.

"Uh…" Karin just looked at Jed. She had never been good at extemporaneous responses. Why hadn't they planned this out?

Jed put his arm around her, pulling her tightly to his side. "Not much to tell," he said. "She just healed my broken heart."

The woman looked worried. "You're a transplant patient?"

That threw him and he stared at her. Karin closed her eyes. Lordy, another thing they'd never talked about.

Karin forced a laugh and slipped her arm around his waist. "Heavens, no," she said. "It was only a figure of speech. Jed's never been a patient of mine."

He planted a quick kiss on her cheek. "Dr. Karin?" he whispered.

She raised her eyebrows in silent response. Was that a problem? Was he one of those men who was only attracted to women who were in a lower pay range?

Not that his preference in women mattered one single bit. She shifted her position to inch away from him. She had no idea where that thought had come from.

"They met at a restaurant," Lissa chimed in.

That stopped Karin's breathing. Lissa wouldn't—

"Daddy swept her off her feet," the girl went on, giving Karin a reassuring smile. "It's 'cause he's so handsome and strong."

Karin slowly let her breath out.

"I was mesmerized by her beauty," Jed said. "Couldn't take my eyes off her."

"Isn't that the sweetest thing?" someone said with a contented sigh.

"So romantic."

"Oh, our food's here," Marge called out.

"We'd better let you all eat then."

"You can catch us later, Fran," Marge went on. "We'll be at the football game this afternoon, or drop in at the bar tonight. I'm having a little open house for these two. Then you can make them tell you all about their wonderful romance."

Karin gave her mother a wide-eyed stare. Football game? Open house? When were they going to be left alone? Not that she wanted to be left alone with *Jed*...

"Stop worrying," the old woman said softly to Jed. "She's fine."

Jed took one last glance into the bedroom at Lissa sound asleep on the bed, Marge's black cat cuddled up close to her. Lissa looked so peaceful, so content. This vacation was already doing her a world of good. He couldn't let anything happen to spoil it.

The cat opened one eye to glare at him so Jed closed the bedroom door as silently as he could. He'd hoped to have a talk with Lissa, plan out their week and make sure she wasn't taking this whole masquerade too seriously. But he guessed that wasn't going to be tonight.

"I appreciate you staying up here with her, ma'am," Jed said.

"She's such a sweetheart," the old woman—Aunty Em—said. "It's a treat to get to know her."

Jed had thought Karin was joking when she'd introduced Penny's grandmother as Aunty Em. But apparently not, since Marge had told him a few minutes ago that Lissa had gone up to bed, and that Aunty Em was going to baby-sit. He guessed the whole town called her that.

"You know who she reminds me of?" Aunty Em said.

Jed stiffened, his blood turning cold. Lissa had been recognized. They'd gone all day without anyone even looking twice at her and he'd stopped being careful. He'd relaxed and that had been his mistake. But maybe he could appeal to the old woman's sense of—

"Karin," Aunty Em went on. "Oh, I know they don't look anything alike, but Lissa's just like Karin was as a little girl. Before she learned to hide her feelings from everybody."

Karin? Relief washed over him, and he hoped it didn't show. "She hides her feelings?" Jed asked idly, only half in the conversation. Lissa hadn't been recognized. So they still had a chance at a real vacation.

Aunty Em laughed and patted his arm. "Oh, I'm sure she doesn't hide them from you. But from others she does. You must have noticed."

The pause in her conversation jerked Jed back to the present. "Oh, yes, of course, ma'am." He edged toward the door. "Guess I'd better get back downstairs."

She waved him off. "You just go take care of Karin. If ever a lady deserved a little cosseting, it's her."

Jed was tempted to ask her questions about Karin's life, but he didn't need to know any more than he already did. Knowing would only lead to helping and that would lead to involvement that neither of them wanted. He nodded to Aunty Em and made his way back to the door. Besides, seeing as how he and Karin were "engaged," he shouldn't have to ask a stranger about his fiancée's past.

He left the second-floor apartment above the bar with a brisk step that slowed once Aunty Em could no longer see or hear him. And the farther he got down the stairs, the slower his descent. Half the town must be here at Marge's. He and Karin hadn't had a moment alone since this morning. And at the rate the night was going, it would be tomorrow morning before they had another one.

They'd never gotten his car, or his and Lissa's luggage. They'd never gone over the basic stories of how and when they met. They didn't even know simple facts about each other, like where they lived or how they earned a living. Now, he didn't mind doing a bit of bluffing, but even the simplest scam needed a little preparation. Maybe he could do some acting and get Karin to take a walk with him. They could firm up their story.

"Hey, there's the man of the moment," someone called out, voices dragging Jed back into the bar.

Smile in place, he made his way through the crowd playing pool and the group gathered around the buffet table, still working on the remains of dinner.

"Congratulations," someone called to him.

"Nice lady you're getting there," someone else said.

He smiled and nodded, shaking hands as he went along. His eyes searched the crowd though, looking for Karin. He found her almost instantly. She was sitting at a booth along the far wall—on which hung about a hundred cowboy hats in all sizes and colors—with her friends Heather, Alex and Dorothy. The other three were laughing and talking and Karin was joining in, but the laughter didn't seem to have melted her tensions and somehow she appeared to be holding herself apart from them.

He took a deep breath, tightened the cinch in his mind and walked over to the booth. "Howdy." He took a deep breath and added, "Darlin'."

She looked up, her cheeks suddenly flushed and her eyes betraying a startled, wary look. "Hi." She seemed to push herself forward. "Sweetheart."

Alex laughed. "Wow, what passion, Karin," he teased. "If we didn't have proof to the contrary, I'd think this guy was a stranger."

"Yeah, and where's your ring?" Dorothy asked.

"Oh, leave her alone," Heather scolded. "Not everyone's comfortable sharing their feelings in front of people. And maybe they haven't had a chance to get a ring yet."

A ring? Jed hadn't even thought of that. "It's on order," he said, "we had to get it sized."

Karin blushed a deep red as he slid into the booth next to her. The lies made him uncomfortable and he hurried to change the subject.

"Lissa was sound asleep," he told Karin as if she'd been waiting for the news. "Didn't even wait for me to tuck her in."

"She had a long day," Karin said.

Her hand was right there near his, and he could almost feel her straining to take his hand. He slid his arm around her shoulder and gave her a slight hug.

"But one of her best in ages," he said. "Your mom's been wonderful."

"She's always wanted grandchildren," Karin said, a painful stiffness in her voice.

Jed grinned widely as he patted her stomach. "Hey, we aim to please."

The others laughed while Karin froze slightly, then tried to join in. Her eyes looked confused, almost angry, but he could feel her fighting her response. If she wanted others to believe they were in love, she was going to have to get used to his touch. Another thing they needed to discuss.

He bent over and brushed a kiss onto her cheek. "What do you say we take a walk?" he said. "Then I think you need to get to bed. You've had a long day, too."

"Hey, I don't need—" Karin stopped abruptly and then found a smile. "A walk would be nice."

"Well, just tell us if we're in the way," Dorothy said with a laugh. "We don't mind."

Suddenly she stopped. A policeman had come over to their table.

Jed felt a moment's uneasiness. What they were doing might be stretching the truth a bit, but it wasn't against the law.

"Toto," Alex said. "You finally get off duty?"

"Toto?" Jed repeated. First Aunty Em, then Dorothy and now Toto?

Alex laughed as he moved closer to Heather. Dorothy frowned at the space suddenly next to her but moved down, leaving room at the end of the seat.

"Tom Tollinger," the policeman said, extending his hand to Jed.

"Ah, I see where the Toto comes from," Jed said as he let go of Karin and got to his feet. He took Toto's hand and shook it. "Jed McCarron."

"It comes from his name and the fact that he dated Dorothy," Heather pointed out.

"Ages ago," Dorothy said.

"Long before she moved to Paris," Toto agreed as he sat down, a careful distance from Dorothy.

"Speaking of Paris," Heather said. "Toto was planning a trip there."

"You were?" Dorothy asked. "Why?"

"Why not?" Toto asked with a shrug as he got back to his feet. "Hey, I'm hungry. I'm going to grab a bite to eat, then I want to hear all about this engagement."

Jed had been watching the byplay with interest. Toto looked at Dorothy like a man eaten up with love, and Dorothy hardly looked at Toto at all—another sure sign of love. But mention of the engagement reminded him of the dangers present.

"Think you're going to have to wait on that," Jed said, getting to his feet. He reached out for Karin's hand. "I'm taking the little mama for a walk and then putting her to bed."

"Oh, really?" someone said with a laugh.

"Don't read anything into it," Karin said as she slid out of the booth. Her smile was wide but her eyes were glittering. "This cowboy's not used to late hours. He's pretty useless once the sun goes down."

"There's a challenge if I ever heard one," Alex said.

Jed took Karin's hand and with a wave at the others, led her through the crowd and out the back door.

"So I'm useless after sundown, am I?" he asked once they were alone in the darkness.

"Anybody is who calls me little mama," she pointed out.

"Well, you aren't very big and you are a mama."

"Not yet I'm not."

"Sure you are," he said. "You may not have a baby in your arms yet, but you sure are a mama."

She turned away and started to walk down the block. "I thought you wanted to take a walk. Or were you just in a mood to lecture?"

He frowned at her. It was dark and shadowy but he could see her figure in the patches of street light. He could also see that there were bunches of cornstalks lined up against the buildings along the block.

He caught up to Karin. "What's with all the cornstalks?" he asked. "Somebody planning on an early Halloween?"

"It's for the festival," she said and stopped walking to look around them. "We do a traveling production of *The Wizard of Oz* and this block will be made into the Scarecrow's cornfield."

"So the whole town is the set for the play?"

"Well, downtown and its surrounding area is. Centennial Park is the forest," she said, waving toward the park he could see in the next block. "Munchkinland is two blocks over, near the library, and Emerald City is by the train station."

"The streets don't look like they're yellow brick."

"They will by next weekend. We have a whole crew of volunteers that will paint the bricks on. My mother works on that committee."

He glanced down the street toward the park, then back the other way toward the library. That was a lot of street to paint. ''This town really takes this seriously. What's the connection to the book? Did the author live here or something?''

''No real connection.'' She started walking again. ''It used to be the play that the junior high put on each year and the festival grew out of that.''

''So the junior-high kids star in the traveling production?''

''Oh, no. The junior high moved on to other plays ages ago. This one belongs to the festival now. We take turns acting in the play, and anybody who wants can be an extra. We have a narrator, so there really are no lines to learn.''

''And is Glinda in the play, too?''

''Afraid so.'' Her steps got brisker as she turned a corner. ''Look, you didn't want to take a walk to learn the history of the Oz festival.''

''Actually I thought we needed to plan some things out,'' he said. ''I've managed to steer clear of answering questions today, but we aren't always going to be that lucky.''

She sighed and slowed her steps a bit. ''You're right. And there'll be no narrator to guide us over the tricky parts, will there?''

''We've sort of covered how we met,'' he said. ''What about your profession—you're a surgeon?''

''Cardiac specialist,'' she said. ''At Rush Presbyterian in Chicago.''

''Sounds impressive.''

''I worked hard to get where I am.''

Her words sounded defensive but her voice wasn't.

They walked for a few minutes in silence, passing a bakery and a hardware store. The sidewalks were wider here, with no cornstalks awaiting placement. Nothing really to remind anyone of the festival.

It seemed to chase the shadows from Karin's mood. "So," she said. "I need to know more about you. Just what does a cowboy do?"

"I'm not so much a cowboy these days," he said. "I used to work the rodeo circuit."

"Isn't rodeo life dangerous?" she asked.

He shrugged. "You can make good money if you're good."

"Were you?"

"Pretty fair. Was the national champion bull rider three years ago. Put away a good store toward a ranch. Another couple of years even half as good and Wendy and I figured we could buy a little spread in the mountains."

"And did you?"

"Buy a little spread?" He shook his head. "Had to quit the circuit when she died."

"I guess it would be hard to drag Lissa around with you."

"And all the psychologists said not to change her routine so I quit and found work near home. I work with an animal trainer in Hollywood. We train horses for work in movies and TV shows."

"And still dream of your ranch?"

He shrugged. "No, ma'am. It was Wendy's and my dream. I can't seem to carry it on my own."

Somehow his hand had found its way into hers and they walked along, pulling on each other's strength. It was a pleasant night, he realized, and this was a pleasant little town. Those were the same stars overhead that he saw in Los Angeles but they seemed brighter here, more available to wish on and less likely to fall.

"How did she die, if you don't mind me asking?" Karin asked softly.

"Car accident," he said. "Couple of teenagers had been drinking after school. They missed a curve and hit her head-on. Both cars totaled. Everybody was killed."

He felt Karin wince. "I'm sorry," she said.

"Me, too. She was a good woman. Deserved a long life."

"Who doesn't?" she said.

He looked at her. "I guess you see a lot of cases that you could say that about," he said.

She nodded as they headed back to the bar. "Too many."

"Must get you down," he said. "Or do you get used to it?"

"You don't think about it," she said. "You do your best and work your hardest and give your patients everything you have to give, and then you turn them back to their primary-care physicians and pray for the best."

Somehow he doubted it was that simple, but a car was pulling away from the curb up ahead and people were yelling and waving and honking their horn. It was a good diversion.

Karin leaned into him suddenly. "I think it would be a good idea for you to kiss me."

Chapter Five

"Now?" Jed asked. The car pulled away. In a moment, it would be too far away for anyone in it to see them. "It's too dark."

"This is Chesterton," she pointed out with an exasperated sigh as she stepped closer to him. "Everyone's got infrared vision."

They were in the shadows of the building and all he could see was a blurry silhouette, but the night did nothing to hide her sweet scent. The soft late-summer air seemed to magnify her allure.

He put his arms around her waist. She moved against him and he could feel the slight thickness where the baby lay inside her. Something stirred within him. He leaned down and kissed her gently on the lips.

It was just going to be a quick kiss, a kiss for show, a kiss to convince anyone watching that this was a real relationship. He'd maybe hold it for the count of three.

But her lips were so soft and her body felt so good in his arms that he missed a count, or two, or three. By the time they broke apart, he desperately needed air.

"Well, that should do the trick," Karin said, her voice as wobbly as his knees.

"Yeah." He was gasping for air, fighting a racing heart.

"Think we can skip the bar and just go upstairs?" she asked, gazing wistfully at the soft glow of lights emanating from the apartment.

But those same lights she was drawn to represented something torturous and painful for Jed—another night in the same bedroom as her. Still, she was probably exhausted.

"Why don't you go on up?" he suggested. "I'm going to take another little walk, I'll be in soon. Leave the door unlocked, okay?"

"Silly," she said. "This is Chesterton. The doors are always unlocked."

Toto reread the newspaper article for the fourth time and still had no idea what it said. He put the paper down with a sigh. Junior had been sleeping on the sofa but opened one eye and gave his tail a tentative wag.

Toto felt like the former police dog could read his mind, but he was not admitting where his thoughts really were. "I think you would like Jed," he told Junior. "He seemed like a nice guy. Though he and Karin don't quite feel like a couple. She seems almost ill-at-ease around him."

The dog lifted his head so that he was looking at Toto with both eyes, as if to say he wasn't fooled. Toto frowned.

"Yes, all right. Dorothy was there, too. She looked

wonderful. Paris is obviously agreeing with her. People were fussing over her as much as they were over new-lyweds Heather and Alex or Karin and Jed, and she was loving every minute of it. I could tell. Are you happy now?''

Junior got to his feet, gave himself a good hearty shake and then trotted into the foyer. Toto frowned after him. What was he doing?

Junior yipped twice, and as Toto was getting up out of his chair, the doorbell rang. By the time Toto got to the door, Junior was frantic with excitement.

Toto's heart sped up a degree. There was only one person that Junior reacted to like this. Toto pulled open the door.

Sure enough, it was Dorothy.

''Hi,'' she said. ''It's not too late to drop in, is it?''

Too late? It was never too late to have her around. ''No, not at all.'' He opened the screen door. ''Come on in.''

Once she'd greeted Junior and endured the dog's ex-uberance, she came into the living room and looked around. ''You're starting to settle in.''

Toto nodded. He'd bought the house about a month ago with the secret hope that he and Dorothy would make it their home, but things hadn't worked out that way. ''This is the only room I've painted so far,'' he said. ''It didn't need much other work.''

''It's nice,'' she said and sat on the sofa.

Junior sat next to her, half lying across her lap in obvious adoration. Toto just sat back down in his easy chair.

''So how have you been?'' he asked. ''Is Paris what you hoped for?''

''It's fine,'' she said, petting Junior. ''It's a big city,

of course. So it's noisy. And it took a little longer to find a job than I had expected.''

Why had he asked that? She thought he was missing her and felt she had to downplay her happiness. He had to assure her it was all right to love Paris. That it was all right not to regret leaving here. And him.

''I think big cities have an energy about them that's exciting,'' he said.

She stopped petting the dog and gave Toto an odd look. ''You do?''

''Sure.'' Hopefully, she didn't remember all the times he'd vowed he would never live in one. ''They make you feel more alive.''

''I guess.'' Junior whined and she went back to petting him.

The dog's groveling was annoying. Or was he just feeling jealous? No, that was crazy. He wasn't jealous of Junior. He was irritated that the dog wasn't doing his part. They needed to convince Dorothy that she was allowed to be happy in Paris.

''I heard you talking at Marge's this evening,'' Toto said. ''That café you said you have breakfast at each morning sounded great. Munchkin's Doughnuts won't ever taste the same for me.''

''Munchkin's apple fritters are pretty good.''

''But not on the same level as freshly baked croissants.'' He laughed, just to show her how great he thought her new life was. ''Though maybe a bunch of us will petition Munchkin's to add croissants to the menu. I wasn't the only one wishing that café was around here.''

''Oh, no?''

''Hey, we're all proud of you and a little envious,

too. They tell you about the junior high adding two more sections of French I?''

"Yeah.'' She didn't sound overly excited.

"And that the South Bend paper did a story about it?''

She looked startled. "About adding sections of French I?''

"About the difference your leaving made to the town. Georgia put up a map of Paris in the library and marked the spot where you live. The Pancake House added quiche to their menu and called it Dorothy's Dinner. Even the liquor store's started stocking more French wine.''

"That's crazy. Other people have left town and no one noticed.''

"They moved away,'' he said. "You followed a dream. Most people don't have the guts to do that.''

"I had no idea anyone was paying that close attention to what I did.'' She looked away for a moment, gazing around the room as if drinking in the details. When she turned back to him, her eyes were shadowed. "Heather said you were thinking of coming to Paris.''

He stared at her a moment, his stomach twisting in sudden knots. He couldn't tell her about the silly bet he'd made with Heather, based on the crazy notion that Dorothy would welcome his visit.

"Oh, that.'' He laughed off her question. "There's an international law enforcement convention in Paris next month and I thought about going. But then I got tickets to the Notre Dame–Michigan game for that weekend. Can't pass up a football game like that.''

"No, I guess not.'' She got to her feet. "Well, I'd better be going. I just wanted to say hi.''

"Glad you dropped by," he said. "Are you staying for the festival?"

She nodded. "Got a much better airfare if I stayed a week."

"I see."

He walked with her to the door. Junior was whining at her departure and Toto wished he could whine, too. She was only staying because of a deal on her airline tickets. This wasn't home anymore.

"Well, take care," he said as he opened the door for her. "I expect I'll see you around."

"Probably." She brushed his cheek with her lips. "Good night."

Toto closed the door after her, but didn't— couldn't—move for ages. He thought his heart had broken when she'd left for Paris—but now he was finding it was breaking all over again.

Jed woke to a luscious mixture of scents. Jasmine? Sweet autumn? Angel breath? Cocoa? And to the sight of Karin's bare slender legs just an arm's length away. She was standing, her back to him as she got some clothes out of the dresser.

Jed just lay there, unmoving, as his gaze slid from her trim ankles, over her tight calves, past those sensitive spots behind her knees and up the gentle swelling of her thighs. A fire exploded inside him and he took a deep breath, then turned over so his back was to her. She was wearing shorts under the long T-shirt she slept in, but still…

He needed to go someplace where he could breathe.

"Oh, you're awake," she said. "Bet it was the smell of the chocolate-chip cookies that woke you up, right?"

Now that she mentioned it, he did recognize the heavy smell of chocolate in the air. But that hadn't been what had woken him up. No, it had been something much deeper and more elemental. Her nearness.

"Yeah, that was it all right," he said and pulled the sheet higher.

He had vowed last night in his solitary walk that he was not going to get involved. That he was not going to feel anything during this masquerade. He was doing it to help Lissa, that was all.

So what happens the very next day? Just sensing Karin's presence near him starts him on fire with desire. Obviously on fire.

Glancing over his shoulder, he saw that she was still looking at some things hanging in the closet. Which made this a good time to hustle into the bathroom and a cold shower. He took a calming breath. He'd spring out of bed, grab his jeans off the back of the desk chair, and holding them in front of the running shorts he was wearing, run like a house afire. He took another breath, tensed his muscles and got ready to spring like a mountain lion leaping for his prey.

But mountain lions rarely had to contend with the overhanging corner of that stupid desk. Jed jumped up and—rammed his head into it.

"Oh, damn." He grabbed his head and sank back on the bed.

"Did you bump your head?" Karin asked sharply. "I told you to move your bed."

"I hate people who have to say 'I told you so,'" he said through gritted teeth. Jeez, he really hit himself good. "That smarts."

"I'm taking a look at it this time," Karin said, her

voice sounding more concerned. She knelt on the edge of his bed.

That was all he needed, her right next to him on the bed. The bump to his head had settled down other parts of him, but he couldn't guarantee they'd stay settled.

"I'm okay," he insisted, trying to get up. "It hurt for a few seconds and now it's fine."

She pulled on his arm to get him back down. "Oh, stop being a baby and let me look at it."

"I'm not being a baby," he cried, shrugging from her touch as if it scalded. "It just doesn't hurt anymore."

"So it's no big deal if I take a look," she said. She put her hand on his shoulder.

He stopped. The touch of her hand paralyzed him in the strangest ways. Because it sent a jolt of awareness through him, like being hit by lightning. Because all he knew was a sweet desire to feel that touch all over him.

He suspected she wasn't feeling similar hungers, though, for she scooted over to kneel in front of him, feeling his head with her fingertips. He tried to close his eyes and breathe normally. He tried to remember she was a doctor.

But all he could do was watch her. Watch the fullness of her breasts so close to him. Breathe in the soft scent of her cologne. Know that he could, oh so easily, slip his hands around her waist.

"It looks okay. A little contusion but nothing serious."

"I told you I was fine," he said, his voice thready and weak. His heart was racing, his body felt feverish.

She sank back on her heels. "I thought you didn't like people who said, 'I told you so.'"

She was still too close to him. He could barely think, just feel. And he felt too much. "Karin, this is not a good idea," he said. Groaned almost.

"What isn't?" she asked, a look of worry flashing through her blue eyes. "You mean the engagement?"

His body wanted her so badly, he was afraid to move. "You and me here," he said.

She looked at him, comprehension coming slowly, then in a rush as her cheeks blazed red. "Oh." Her hands flew up to cover her cheeks. "I'm sorry. I wasn't thinking. I'm so bad at all this."

Her embarrassment was more than he could bear. He reached over and took her hands in his. "It's okay, darlin'," he said softly. "Relax. No harm's done."

But tears welled up in her eyes. "I am so dumb at times. You'd think I'd have learned my lesson," she said, waving down at her belly.

"Oh, hush now," Jed said, pulling her into his arms. He was playing with fire, he knew, but he couldn't stand to hear her blaming herself. "Stop putting yourself down."

"Excuse me," Marge said with a loud cough. "I did knock, but I guess you were a little busy."

They flew apart like guilty lovers and turned toward the door.

"Jed hit his head," Karin said quickly.

Lissa peeked around Marge with a frown. "Is he okay? Are you gonna have to go to the hospital, Daddy?"

"I'm fine, sweetie," he said.

"Don't worry, honey, your dad's okay," Marge said, putting her hands on Lissa's shoulders. "Now go box the rest of the cookies."

Once Lissa was gone, Karin's mother turned toward

Jed. "Your little girl needs to talk to you when you get a chance."

"Glad to," Jed said. Damn. He was really screwing up. He was letting himself get all rattled by Karin and then not being there for Lissa when she needed him.

"I'll go shower," Karin said as she climbed off the bed. "Unless you want the bathroom first."

"No, go ahead. I need to talk to Lissa." He pulled on his jeans over his shorts and went out into the kitchen where Lissa was counting cookies.

She was wearing clothes from her overnight bag— tan slacks and her favorite red blouse. Her hair had been washed and curled and she looked all too close to the Lissa that appeared in the Crunchy Flakes ads. But maybe she had something planned for the two of them that wouldn't put them around too many people.

"Have you had breakfast?" Jed asked.

Lissa rolled her eyes. "We've been up for ages, Dad."

"Since the crack of dawn," Marge added.

It wasn't that late, but he just ignored the ribbing. "What's on our agenda for today?"

Lissa frowned at him a little nervously. "I'm going to school."

"School?" Jed shook his head.

"Ginger's invited Lissa to come to school with her," Marge explained. "You met the Tompkins family at Penny's wedding. Everything's been cleared with the principal and the teacher."

"And I'm bringing cookies," Lissa said.

Jed was having trouble comprehending. It was like that time in Calgary when the bull he was riding threw him into the front-row seats. "You want to go to school on your vacation?"

"We were going to check with you yesterday," Marge said. "But we couldn't find you."

"And I said we didn't have to check," Lissa said. "'Cause you said it was my vacation and I could do anything I wanted."

"Oh. Yeah, right." He had said that. But he hadn't expected she was going to up and leave him.

"We better get going, Grandma," Lissa said. "I don't want to be late."

"Sure, honey. I'll go get my purse."

While Marge went off into the other room, Lissa came over to sit next to Jed. "You sure you don't mind?" she asked.

That worried look was creeping back into her eyes. Her voice was just a touch hesitant. "Of course not," he assured her quickly. "Whatever you want." He lowered his voice. "But wear one of your hats so no one recognizes you."

She got to her feet, shaking her head with a smile. "Nobody will. I asked Grandma for Crunchy Flakes for breakfast and she said nobody eats them here."

That awoke another worry. "Lissa, about this whole Grandma—"

She frowned at him. "I know it's just make-believe," she whispered. "Jeez, Dad. Give me a break."

Marge came back into the room. "You ready?" she asked Lissa. "Got the cookies?"

"Yes and yes." Lissa grabbed up the box of treats and a baseball cap from a hook near the door. "Bye, Dad."

Marge looked over at Jed and shook her head. "Hey, cheer up, cowboy. Now you and Karin'll have some time alone together."

Just what he needed.

* * *

Karin was in no hurry to get out of the shower. She needed the time to get herself back in control. She was having the strangest reactions to being around Jed. Her heart raced when she heard his voice, and when she'd woken up this morning and lay watching him sleep, she felt her body temperature rise as if she had a fever.

She was sorry she'd started this whole thing. It had seemed so simple when the idea had come to her, but it was getting more and more complicated by the moment. Maybe she should just call it quits.

By the time she was drying herself off, she'd decided that was what she should do. Definitely call it off. It had been a mistake. Unfair to Jed and Lissa. Wrong to lead her mother on. And much too much for her own nerves. And today would be the perfect time. She had to go back into Chicago to check on a few patients, so she'd tell him it was over and drop him off at his car. By the time she got home later this evening, he and Lissa would be gone.

But then Karin went into the kitchen and found her mother back from taking Lissa to Ginger's house. Karin couldn't discuss this while her mother was here, so she ate some breakfast and waited until she and Jed left.

Of course, then she couldn't say anything until Jed drove them out of Chesterton—just in case someone who could read lips was passing by.

"I need to go into Chicago and check on some patients," she said once they were out in open farm country. "We'll pick up your car and then I'll go on from there. You can go on back to Chesterton."

"Why don't I just go with you?" he said.

She needed time alone, that was why. Not that she could say that. "What for? You'd only end up sitting around the hospital lobby for hours. And I feel fine. No problem driving."

"Well, it's either sitting around a hospital lobby or sitting around Chesterton," he pointed out. "At least in Chicago no one's going to catch me in a lie. Besides, I've been thinking. I'm not sure it would look right for me to have my own car. I thought I'd get the luggage, then call the rental company and have them come get it from the oasis."

"Why?" she asked. She'd been busy trying to find the right words to call the whole thing off, and his words took her by surprise.

"We're supposed to be a couple. Why would we have separate cars?"

"My trips to check on patients would be one reason," she said and then cleared her throat. "Actually, I've been thinking, too. I think maybe we should forget this whole thing."

He flashed her a startled look as he pulled into the tollway oasis parking lot, but said nothing until he parked the car. "Call it off?" he repeated. "How in the world can we do that?"

She was more prepared with the whys than the hows. "It's just not fair to you and Lissa," she said. "And I'm not sure it's all that kind to lead my mother on, either."

He turned, leaning on the steering wheel as he frowned at her. "What do we say? That it was all a lie or that we fought and called off our engagement?" He sounded confused and a little impatient.

His reaction was actually rather surprising. She

would have thought he would jump at the chance to be free of her and the lie.

"Does it matter?" she said. "Whatever works."

"I don't see how anything will," he pointed out. "Either way, I come out as the villain and it would mean the end of Lissa's vacation."

Karin hadn't thought of that. "Not necessarily," she said slowly. "We can say it was all my doing. No one will blame you."

He gave her a look. "No thank you, ma'am. No woman is going to take the blame for my foolishness."

"Oh, stop going all noble on me," she snapped. "This isn't working. Neither of us is comfortable around the other. We can't do half the things we want to because we're supposed to be a couple. And we are so totally incompatible that no one in their right mind would believe it anyway."

"Lissa's having a good time," he said.

"She still can. Telling the truth isn't going to change anything."

"You can't really believe that," he said. "I may be from the big city, but I can guess how things work in a small town. We'd suddenly be real strangers, not just townsfolk they hadn't met yet. There'd be no invitations for Lissa to go to school with them."

This wasn't going the way Karin thought it would. "So you do other things," she said.

"We had a bargain," he said. "And I'm holding you to your end."

He got out of the car then, taking the car keys with him as if he thought she might drive away without him. Hardly. This discussion wasn't over with. She got out of the car, too, slamming the door behind her, and hurried after him.

"I'll still talk to Lissa as Glinda," she said.

He was unlocking the trunk of his rental car, but glanced her way. "If we call this off, we can't stay around that long."

He really was making this much more difficult than it had to be. "Of course you can. You can even come to events as my guest."

He grabbed their suitcases from the trunk. "It's less than a week," he said after she'd shut the trunk lid. "What's the big deal?"

"It's the principle of the thing," she tried to explain as she followed him back to her car.

His look said he didn't buy that. And to be honest, it was an awfully weak argument. But she couldn't exactly tell him that her heart beat faster near him. That she felt quivery inside when she heard his soft drawl. It was all due to her crazy pregnant hormones, she knew. But there had to be a better argument she could use.

"Hello!" someone called out.

They both looked up to see the waitress from the oasis restaurant bearing down on them, a huge grin on her face.

"It's you two!" she cried. "I thought it was."

"Howdy, ma'am," Jed said politely, tipping his hat.

The woman stopped in front of them, her face taking on a serious look. "How are you?" she asked Karin, her eyes getting wide as they traversed the full length of her. "My gosh, you're gonna be a mama. The baby's okay, isn't it?"

"Yes, we're fine," Karin said. It was kind of the woman to care, but Karin really wanted to be gone. She and Jed still needed to get this thing settled. "I hope that there wasn't too much damage done here."

The woman waved her hand. "Enough, but the storm hasn't hurt business any. Actually maybe helped it." She turned to Jed. "Hey, some reporter's been looking for you. She heard how you saved this lady here, and wanted to do a story about you and your little girl."

Publicity was one of the last things in the world Karin wanted, but she was surprised at the sudden stillness in Jed, at the fleeting sense of panic she felt in the air.

"Too bad," he said with a forced laugh. "Guess we missed our chance at fame."

"Oh, no," the waitress said. "It wasn't a story about the storm, but about heroes. I've got her number. She wanted me to call if I see you again. Where you folks staying?"

"Just passing through," Jed said quickly. "Afraid she'll have to find somebody else—a real hero—for her story."

He tossed the luggage into the back of the Jeep and went around to Karin's door. "Coming, darlin'?" he asked.

Karin had a moment's realization that she could use this to her advantage, that she could keep quiet about where he was in exchange for him agreeing to end their pretend engagement. But she couldn't.

"Sure, honey," she said and smiled at the waitress. "Thanks for your interest." She got into the car.

He backed out of the parking spot. "So on to Chicago?"

She shrugged. "Just head west on the tollway," she said. "I'll tell you when to get off."

Jed didn't say anything else as they drove away from the oasis. Karin just stared out the window at the passing neighborhoods and tried to figure out why she wasn't more upset. She should be angry at him for refusing to end their fake engagement. She should be tense that they would be found out. So why did she feel all flushed and warm? Why was her heart beating so? It was these damn hormones.

Jed wasn't used to this. His insides were all tied up in knots and he couldn't think straight. That had been a close call back there at the oasis with the waitress. All he needed was some reporter to track them down and everything would be ruined—Lissa's vacation and Karin's face-saving engagement.

He followed Karin's directions from the tollway to an expressway and then onto the city streets, stewing the whole way. He had to be more careful. He had to watch his every step. He was letting the calm and peaceful environment of Chesterton suck him in.

"You probably think I'm nuts," he finally said with a short laugh. "I guess most folk would jump at the chance to be branded a hero."

"It's your decision," Karin said.

But he barely heard her. "And then me insisting on keeping up this pretense, probably doesn't make much sense to you, does it?"

"Well, that doesn't, no." She sighed loudly. "I don't get that at all. Turn left up here."

He did as she instructed then didn't say much, indecision bouncing around in his stomach. He was sure he could trust her. She wouldn't tell anyone who Lissa was, but somehow he couldn't say the words. It would be telling too much, opening up too big a part of him.

"It's just that Lissa's everything to me," he said

slowly. "She took her mother's death real hard and I want her to have the vacation she's been dreaming of."

"She's been dreaming of going to school on her vacation? Turn right at the light."

He slowed down for the turn. "She was dreaming of being part of the town like her mom was when she lived here," he said. "I never figured she'd get more than a tourist experience, but luck smiled on us and she's getting more. I can't be the one to take that away from her."

He drove down a few blocks, feeling as if he was back in Los Angeles and choking. Traffic wasn't bad, but it was just the sense of everyone hurrying around in their own little worlds, never touching or laughing, that got to him.

"You can pull into this parking garage up here." Karin handed him a plastic key card. "The first two levels are reserved for physicians."

He pulled into the dark concrete structure, and he missed the sunlight immediately. It was lightless like his world after Wendy died. Then he spotted a patch of sunshine pouring in over a half wall. He drove into a spot there.

"Do you still miss your wife?" Karin asked as he turned off the engine.

The question surprised him, but he just shrugged. "No more than if someone tore my heart out."

"It's just that you hide your grieving well," she said.

"I don't deal the cards in this life," he pointed out and went around to open her door. "All I can do is play them. It's all any of us can do. It's what you had to do after your boyfriend left you and the baby."

She didn't meet his eyes as she got out of the car,

as if the subject was too painful for her. "It wasn't exactly like that," she said. Her voice was brusque, her manner stiff. "He wasn't my boyfriend. He was more like an...an experiment."

"An experiment?"

She'd started across the parking garage, keeping her back to him so he couldn't see her face. Just the rigid set of her shoulders.

He caught up with her. "What kind of experiment?"

She stopped and turned to face him. "If you must know," she said quietly. "I wanted to see if I had a heart."

Chapter Six

"If you had a heart?" Jed repeated. "What in the world are you talking about?"

Karin had started walking again. "Growing up I was teased that I didn't have a heart. After a while I began to wonder if people were right. I never fell in love like all the other girls, like other women."

"That doesn't mean anything," he said on a hiss. There was something so fragile about the way she held herself. "Maybe you never met the right person."

They'd reached a door and he opened it for her. They were in a hallway of the hospital, lined with offices and the emergency room farther down. The smell of sickness and death and despair came rushing out toward him. On one level they brought back those long hours after Wendy's accident, but on another he was feeling that same despair from Karin at his side.

"There's no timetable for falling in love," he

pointed out quietly. "Just because you haven't, it doesn't mean you can't."

"Oh, come on," she said. "Didn't you fall in love about a dozen times a year in grade school and have some major crushes in high school?"

"So what if I did?"

"I didn't," she said, stopping at a desk to sign in, before continuing down the hall. "It's really kind of funny. I'd be much more suited to play the Tinman than Glinda at the festival."

"That's the craziest thing you've said yet," he snapped.

She stopped at an elevator. "The red line on the floor will take you to the lobby. I'll meet you there when I'm done. I'll be a good couple of hours if you want to take a walk or something."

"I'll plan out the highlights of our torrid romance," he said.

She made a face and got into the elevator. "If I'm going to be later than I expect, I'll leave a message with the lobby receptionist and you could go back to Chesterton."

"I'm not going anywhere without you," he said.

The elevator doors closed on his words and he stood there staring at the smooth metal. The reflection that stared back at him was blurry and indistinct, just the vague hint of a man.

It was true that one of them didn't have a heart, but it wasn't Karin. It was him. He'd given it to Wendy and it had broken when she died. One to a customer and he'd used his up. Karin had hers buried deep underneath a mountain of fears. One day she'd find it and give it away. Hopefully, the jerk she gave it to would appreciate the rarity of the gift.

* * *

Karin didn't want Jed to stay. In fact, she should have told him outright to leave. She could take the South Shore back home when she was done. The train station wasn't far from her mother's place. It would be much better than knowing he was waiting for her.

She even went down to the lobby after checking on her first two patients. She meant to tell him to leave, but somehow it didn't work.

"I'm going to be a while longer," she told him. "Why don't you go?"

He lowered his magazine. "I think I'll just wait here a spell," he said. "No telling how lost I'd get trying to find my way back to Chesterton."

She wasn't fooled by that *shucks, ma'am* cowboy drawl. "I can draw you a map."

"Why don't we just wait a bit?" he said with a smile. "I'm needing to finish this here article anyway so I'm in no hurry."

She looked at what he was reading. *Worldwide News.* "Are you fascinated by the story of Jupiter people landing in New York or the article about the potato that looks like Elvis?"

"Actually, I'm reading this fascinating article about a woman with no heart," he said. "The medical community is astounded."

She was torn between laughing at him and hitting him, but chose neither. "I might have an emergency surgery," she said. "If so, you're going to be stuck here a long time."

"I'll call your mom," he said. "And tell her we'll be late."

The man was so infuriating! She wished she had never met him. As she went stomping back to the elevator, though, she thought about how he had pulled her away from the door at the tollway restaurant the other day, saving her from serious injury. The knowledge made her feel guilty for being rude to him. She would be nicer to him the next time.

Except that was impossible. When she came down an hour later—around lunchtime—he was sitting on the floor, surrounded by a half-dozen kids of all ages. They were enraptured by some rodeo story he was telling them. One little girl was even wearing his cowboy hat.

Karin had to look away and blink back a sudden rush of tears. So what if he was a good and kind man? A great father while her baby wouldn't even have a mediocre one.

She took a deep breath and marched over to where he was holding court. "I'm going to be in surgery for several hours at least. The doctor who was supposed to operate is ill," she told him. "I won't know how long the procedure will take until I get inside. You really should go."

He looked up at her. "And what'll you do?"

"I can take the train."

"It runs all night?"

"I can go to my condo for the night," she pointed out.

He shook his head and playfully pulled the brim of his hat down over the little girl's face. "Nope. I think I'll stay. Lucy here's mom is sick and we want to stay with her until we find out she's okay." He turned to the other kids. "Right, guys?"

"Right, Jed."

"Uh-huh."

"Cowboys don't mind waiting."

He smiled at her as if that settled the matter. "I will call your mom again though and let her know."

"Fine." He just didn't understand she didn't want him here. She turned to go back upstairs.

"Darlin'."

She turned at his soft voice even as she was telling herself that he wasn't talking to her, that he should call her by name. That she was nobody's *darling*. He was on his feet, his eyes serious.

"You work some magic for your emergency, okay?"

She couldn't have spoken to save her life. The belief in her that shone in his eyes overwhelmed her. All she could do was nod and leave.

Luck was with her patient. He only needed double bypass surgery, not triple as they first thought and the surgery went well, no complications. Still, she didn't feel it was safe to leave until he was settled in the cardiac intensive care unit and he was awake.

When she dragged herself down to the lobby, it was dark outside. She was suddenly glad that she didn't have to face the night alone. And that she didn't have to make herself be strong so she could drive home.

She went into the lobby. The kids were gone and a handful of people were sitting in the chairs, staring at the television or reading. Jed was slouched down in a chair by the far wall, legs stretched out in front of him and his hat over his face. It looked as if he was sleeping. She felt so guilty for keeping him here.

"Jed?" she said softly.

He was awake and on his feet in an instant. His eyes looked too alert for someone who just got woken up. Maybe he had been pretending and peeking out at her as she approached. The idea irritated her slightly.

"You look beat, darlin'," he said and slipped an arm around her shoulders. "How'd it go?"

"Fine. I think he's out of danger." She knew she sounded stiff and unfriendly. And his arm around her did feel awfully reassuring. Maybe she was overreacting. She looked around at the sparse crowd in the room. "How's Lucy's mom?"

"Doing better." His voice was thoughtful, as though he really cared. "You ready to go?"

She nodded, suddenly feeling too confused to think. She was tired, but it was more than that. His arm around her shoulders felt just too right. His understanding, his trust, his concern all were somehow vital to her. And what she really wanted was to lie in his arms and let the world disappear for a few hours. Her silly mind was wondering what it would be like to be kissed by him, really and thoroughly kissed.

Heavens, where was she letting her thoughts go? She let him lead her out to the car and sank into the passenger seat with a slow sigh. She was tired, that was all. It was those hormones. They were running amok again. If she stayed quiet and kept her thoughts to herself, this fit would pass. She would lean her head back, close her eyes and—

She sat upright. He'd pulled out of the garage and was driving back to the expressway, finding his way through the maze of one-way streets like a native.

"I thought you couldn't go home because you'd get lost," she said.

"It's dark out now. Cowboys can find their way by the stars."

She groaned and leaned back again. It wasn't worth trying to fight him. He had an answer for everything. She closed her eyes and...and the next thing she knew they were home, pulling into the small parking lot behind the bar.

No, not home. She blinked, trying to wash the sleepy fog from her brain. Back at her mother's place. It hadn't been her home for years now and it certainly never was—and never would be—Jed's home.

"You awake?" Jed asked.

"Of course," she said and proved it by getting out of the car before he could come open her door. "I was just reviewing my day."

"Ah, exactly what I suspected."

She didn't acknowledge his mockery, but slowly went up the stairs to the second floor apartment. The long day had gotten to her more than she wanted to admit. Or was it Jed's presence that had gotten to her? No, it couldn't be that.

"This was actually an easy day," she told him as she reached the back porch. "I've had much worse ones. Ones where I was in surgery all day."

"But that was before," he said. "The further along you get in your pregnancy, the more tired you're going to get."

He was right behind her. So close that his breath tickled the back of her neck. No, it was just her awareness of him, of his nearness. She had to stop imagining things like that!

"Not necessarily. Some women feel fine until they go into labor."

She couldn't afford to let pregnancy weaken her. Just as she couldn't afford to dream there was some attraction between her and Jed. That idea was a demon that needed to be stared down fast.

She turned around. He was closer than she had thought and the backlight more golden and magical.

His eyes seemed to be dark pools of longing that she could drown in. His mouth seemed to invite her touch.

She had all sorts of things to say, all sorts of clever remarks to keep him—and her fanciful thoughts—at a distance. But they vanished like dew under the summer sun. She was only conscious of the need of her lips, the hunger in her hands, the desire of her body to rest against him.

He took a step closer then and she was in his arms. His lips took hers and the moment came alive. She felt a warmth, a wonder explode inside her that spread through every inch of her. His lips wove magic around them both while his hands pulled her closer and closer still.

He was hard and lean and all man. Her softness seemed to fit against him perfectly. Her body—at the beginnings of awkwardness—felt like pure woman. There was a rightness in their embrace, a meeting of opposites, a melding of two puzzle pieces. His lips were whispering the song of the stars to her, lighting a fire within her that wanted no containing. Her hands were bringing a—

The kitchen door swung open and they moved apart as the light from inside flooded over the porch. It brought sanity with a thud. What in the world was she thinking?

"You two giving the neighbors a show?" Marge asked with a laugh. "Sharing a bedroom isn't enough now?"

Oh, Lordy. Karin gulped back the panic rising in her throat. How had she forgotten? She was spending all night with him!

"Are you sure you don't mind, Daddy?"

Jed was trying to think coherently after another

sleepless night. Maybe it was a little selfish, but he'd been counting on a full day of doing things with Lissa to keep him away from Karin—both in his thoughts and in reality. He needed some breathing room. But Lissa wasn't going to provide him with it. He'd found out this morning that she had plans of her own.

"I'm just worried you're going to be recognized," he said. "You know what happened at Albany."

"It's different here," Lissa told him. "I don't think anyone eats Crunchy Flakes or saw me on 'Kid's Korner' last year. And Betsy didn't even know her jeans were 'Lissa's Line' jeans."

"Yeah, but—"

"I took my hat off yesterday and nobody recognized me. It's safe here."

Marge was on the phone, talking to someone from her Yellow Brick Road painting crew. Karin was still sleeping. And Lissa was sitting next to Jed at the kitchen table, carrying such a load of pleading in her face that it near to broke his heart. He reached out and pulled his daughter into a big bear hug on his lap. Like yesterday, she was all dressed up, ready and rarin' to go. And like yesterday, she had a full schedule planned.

"Okay," he said. "You go have a good time. We can do something later."

"But after school we're painting bricks on the library parking lot for the start of the Yellow Brick Road," Lissa pointed out, her voice wobbly with worry. "And then Ginger wants me to come over after dinner to work on our costumes. She was Dorothy last year and said her mom can fix the dress so it fits me, but her shoes are too small so we have to make one of my pairs of shoes all glittery and magic."

Jed smiled at her. "The only problem I see is that you're so busy, I'm gonna forget what you look like."

Lissa wrapped her arms around his neck. "Don't worry, Daddy," she said. "I won't be doing so much stuff when we get back to Los Angeles."

Concern flared up, twisting his stomach. Why did Lissa say "back to Los Angeles" instead of "back home"? Was this a new complication? Or was he over-reacting? "Yeah," Jed agreed slowly, letting his worries out in a slow exhale. "You can't go so many places on your own in a big city."

"I suppose," Lissa said, slipping off his lap. "But mostly I don't want you to be alone all the time. You don't have anyone to play with in L.A., Daddy. But here you've got Karin."

Another concern hit him with a sucker punch to the gut. "You know that's only make-believe, honey. Just pretend for while we're here. Then we go back home to just the two of us." Jed cleared his throat. "Even Dorothy had to go back to Kansas."

"I know. But before she went back, she had a lot of adventures in Emerald City."

Marge came into the kitchen. "You ready, Lissa?"

"Sure, Grandma," Lissa said. "Just let me give Shilah a kiss."

Lissa ran off to find Marge's cat and Marge sank into a chair.

"Having problems with your brick-painting crew?" Jed asked.

She nodded. "Not that I'm complaining, mind you. George got called out to fly a kidney from Muncie to Philadelphia so a little kid can have a transplant. It's a hell of a lot more important than painting bricks, but his going does leave us shorthanded today."

"Why don't I take his place on the crew?" he said. "Might be a way for me to earn my keep."

Lissa came bouncing back into the kitchen, so Marge got to her feet, but her eyes were still on Jed. "Land sakes, cowboy. Just by making my little girl happy, you've more than earned your keep."

"You just tell me what I need to do," he said. He reached down and pulled Lissa into a bear hug. "You have a good day, darlin'."

"You too, Daddy."

Then she skipped out the door. Marge followed her, not exactly skipping too, but there was a definite bounce in her step. Jed sighed.

"Something the matter?"

Jed turned. Karin was in the bedroom doorway. There was something about her in the morning that pulled at his heart. It was a vulnerability in her eyes, a softness in her mouth. It was as if she hadn't put up all her defenses yet and he was catching a glimpse of the real her, feeling as if it was a rare gift she didn't show just anybody. And maybe didn't even mean to show him. Why did that sadden him so?

"No, nothing's wrong," he said. "How are you? Sleep well?"

"Yes, fine." Her eyes narrowed. "Why do you ask?"

Maybe because he had hardly slept at all and could have sworn she was tossing and turning just as much. "No reason. You need to go back into Chicago to check on your patients?"

She hesitated a flickering moment, then went over to make a cup of tea. "No, my partner's going to check on them for me. I've got a bunch of errands I need to run today." She put her cup of water in the microwave, then turned to face him. "If you want the Jeep for something, I'll borrow Mom's car."

He ought to be relieved that they were finally getting some breathing room, but somehow his silly heart was pretending otherwise. "No, I'm going to help your mother on one of the brick-painting crews," he said. "I don't think I'll need a car for anything."

"Okay." The microwave beeped and she got her cup out, plopped a tea bag into it and headed toward the bathroom. "I'm going to shower and get started then. See you later."

"Right. See you later." He watched the door close behind her with a confused heart. If he was so glad to be on his own today, why wasn't he feeling happy?

Later that day, Karin frowned at herself in the mirror. Pink and frilly was not her style. Or more likely, a wise and kindly good witch was not her. "I think this fits fine," she told Heather, in a hurry to get the costume off. "I don't think you need to let it out any more."

Heather gave her a look and went back to making marks along the side seams at the waist. "You are getting larger, you know, not smaller. If it's too tight today, it's not going to fit better for the parade."

"It's only a couple of days."

"And this will only take a couple of minutes." She made the last mark on the fabric and then stood, unbuttoning the tiny buttons all along the back.

Karin stepped out of the dress with relief. She felt more like herself again. It was silly, she knew. The costume was all make-believe, but she didn't feel comfortable in it.

"So I hear you had an emergency surgery yesterday,'' Heather said as she carried the dress over to the sewing table.

"How'd you hear that?" Karin put her shorts and T-shirt back on, avoiding her reflection in the mirror. It was silly, she knew, but she felt more like herself without any visuals. She could pretend that life was as usual and no crises were just around the bend.

"Your mom told Mrs. Fallon and she told Robbie Baker's mother and Robbie announced it to my kindergarten class this morning."

Karin sank into a chair. "I forgot how everything's a big deal in this town. I have emergencies all the time. This was nothing major."

"I bet it was to the guy whose life you saved," Heather pointed out. "How's he doing?"

"Fine. He was alert and feeling good this morning."

Heather had spread the dress out and had started ripping out a seam but stopped to frown at Karin. "You went in to check on him?"

"Of course." Karin felt a twinge of guilt. She hadn't really lied to Jed earlier. She really hadn't *needed* to go into Chicago; she had *wanted* to.

"Did Jed drive you again?" Heather asked.

"No." Karin sat up. "I do know how to drive."

"Yeah, but it must be tiring for someone in your condition. I'm surprised Jed let you."

Karin got to her feet. "Hey, I'm just pregnant, not an invalid, and it's not up to Jed to 'let me' or 'not let me' do something."

"Why am I not convinced Jed would see it that way?" Heather asked with a grin and went back to working on the seam.

Karin went to look at the other costumes hanging in the closet. Heather did such great work; she could do it for a living. Of course, she was a perfect kindergarten teacher, too.

"Jed's really a nice guy," Heather said after a few minutes.

Karin looked at her. "Yeah, he is." Maybe too nice for this pretense.

"It surprised me how nice he is," Heather went on.

Karin wasn't sure what that was supposed to mean. "Why?"

Heather shrugged. "You told me last month that your baby's father was out of your life and not coming back," she said.

Damn, had she? Karin thought back to that day Heather brought her costume into Chicago for a fitting, but couldn't really remember the details.

"Well, he changed his mind," Karin said with an uneasy laugh. She'd never been good at lying.

"Funny. Jed doesn't seem like the sort to turn his back on his child."

Double damn. Why had she ever started this? "Actually, I was the one who broke it off before," Karin said. "You know me, afraid of commitment."

"But you took the leap," Heather said, and getting to her feet, came over and gave Karin a hug. "I am so happy that you are finally willing to risk love. You two are going to be so happy." Then she laughed and patted Karin's belly. "You three. No, you four. Gosh, Karin, when you finally decide to do something, you really do it, don't you?"

Karin tried to laugh, but she couldn't do more than smile slightly. She should tell Heather the truth. She'd understand, and she'd probably help Karin pull off the charade. It would be so great to confide in someone—except Heather would probably tell Alex and they would tell Penny and Brad when they came back from their honeymoon and...

No, it was her secret. Hers and Jed's. "I think I'd better be getting along," Karin said. "You don't need me anymore do you?"

"Nope." Heather put the dress down and walked with Karin to the front door. "Will we see you two at the square dance tonight?"

"The square dance?" Karin remembered that her friends belonged the local square-dance club, but it had never been her style. Not that she did much of any kind of dancing. "I think I'll pass."

"What a shame. I thought it would be something Jed would like."

Karin stopped. "I have no idea if he would or wouldn't."

"He's a cowboy, isn't he? All cowboys like to square-dance."

Maybe Heather was right. The cowboys Karin's mother hooked up with had liked to drink and gamble and spend other people's money, but Jed wasn't like them at all. Maybe he would like to go dancing.

The twinge of guilt played at her again. She owed him for all he was doing for her, and a night doing something he would enjoy would be a start.

"Maybe we will come," Karin said. "Yeah, definitely. Count us in."

"Great."

It would be. It would be a great evening. Jed would have fun.

"Are you sure you don't want to come with us?" Karin asked Lissa as they all left the apartment. "I'm positive there'll be kids your age there."

To be honest, Karin was wishing Lissa would join them. Karin had been getting more and more nervous as the evening approached. She'd only suggested the idea because she thought Jed deserved to have an evening he'd enjoy, but now it was feeling almost like a date. Just the two of them, and her trying to show Jed a good time. If Lissa was along, it would relieve some of that date-like pressure.

But Lissa was shaking her head as she skipped down the steps to the parking lot. "Ginger and Bethany are going to help me with my special shoes this evening. I'm going to be the best Dorothy ever."

"Maybe they'd want to come too," Karin suggested. She hoped she didn't sound too desperate.

Lissa had gotten to the bottom of the steps and turned. "I doubt it. I can't believe that you're going. Daddy—"

"—was just saying how it had been ages since he'd been to a square dance," Jed finished for her. "I hope I'm not too rusty."

Karin felt the jitters in her stomach double and triple as she walked over to the Jeep. Was that what Lissa had been going to say? Jed hadn't seemed reluctant when she'd suggested square dancing. Damn. If she just knew how to read men better. But surely he would have said that he didn't want to go, if he hadn't. It wasn't as though she'd forced this on him.

They all three climbed into the car. Maybe she was letting her doubts creep into her voice and it was affecting everyone. She watched as Jed pulled out of the lot and turned down Calumet, going past the scarecrow's cornfield and past the library and the set of Munchkinland. Down the street, in the churchyard, was the set for Kansas. Where did she belong? In the drab, gray Kansas or colorful, magical Oz? Probably neither.

"Well, I think you're going to miss out on a lot of fun," Karin told Lissa, keeping her voice as perky as possible. "When we tell you what a great time we had, you're going to be sorry."

Jed laughed. "That's telling her, darlin'."

A warm feeling washed over her, taking her by surprise and bringing her nervousness rushing back. "You don't have to call me that in private." She felt somehow duty-bound to say it.

"Oh, he calls everybody that," Lissa said. "Turn up here, Dad."

Everybody? Karin's throat closed up a little. Not that it mattered. She didn't care one way or another.

"Well, not everybody," Jed pointed out.

"Okay, all the ladies," Lissa corrected. "It's the house on the corner up there."

All the ladies. She wasn't exactly part of an elite bunch, was she? Which was fine with her. The very last thing she wanted was for Jed to be developing feelings for her. It was a relief to know he wasn't.

And just to prove she wasn't developing feelings for him, she needed to discuss this too.

"Doesn't calling women darling get confusing?" Karin asked. "How would someone know when you mean it to be special?"

"Oh, you can tell," Lissa said as Jed slowed the car to a stop in front of the corner house. "It sounds different. Thanks, Dad. Have fun, Karin."

"Do you need us to pick you up?" Jed asked.

"Nope." Lissa opened the car door and climbed out. "Bethany's mom is going to drop me off at Grandma's."

"You have a key?"

"Dad." Karin could hear in the girl's voice that she was rolling her eyes. "This is Chesterton. Nobody locks their doors."

She slammed the door and raced up the sidewalk. Two girls were waiting on the porch for her and hurried her inside.

Karin turned to Jed, but found him still watching the door where Lissa had disappeared. His face was open and easy to read for once. Pride, sadness, worry, joy. All in his eyes and the twist of his lips.

"She's having a good time," Karin said softly.

He turned to smile at her. "Yeah, it's working out great."

A twinge of something tugged at her as he pulled the Jeep away from the curb. "Mom's going to miss her," Karin said. "I never imagined how attached she'd get to Lissa."

"Or Lissa to her."

"At least Lissa knows the truth," Karin pointed out. "At times I feel awful for starting this whole pretense."

"Not much we can do now, but play it out to the end," Jed said.

"I know." The thought of its being over seemed to hit her harder than she expected.

She directed Jed down a yellow brick painted road to the VFW hall where the square dance was to be held, determined to push her gloominess into the shadows. She was going to play her part to the hilt and make sure he had fun. They got out of the Jeep and walked into the lobby of the hall.

"Quite a crowd here." She pushed herself a step further. "Darling."

"Darlin'," he said.

That warm flush washed over her again though she knew better this time. "What?" she asked.

"You gotta drop the *g* in *darling*," he said. "Soften the word or it doesn't mean anything."

She thought it didn't mean anything anyway. "Soften?"

"Let me show you." He led her off to the side and put his arms around her waist. "Hello, darlin'," he said as he bent down and kissed her. So softly. Like the summer breeze that made the daisies dance gently in the sunshine. Like—

Damn. This was so unfair that she wanted to cry. He looked as hard as a rock, yet he was as gentle as could be. It was really rotten, she thought as she put her arms around his neck and kissed him back.

"What do think—9.5?" Dorothy said.

"I don't know. The form is good but it's a shade low on passion."

Oh, Lordy! Karin jumped out of Jed's arms, her cheeks on fire. There in the lobby stood Alex, Heather, Dorothy and Toto, grinning at her and Jed.

"What are you guys doing here already?" Karin asked.

"What do you mean 'already,'" Dorothy asked. "The dance is about to start. What are *you* doing, out in the lobby?"

Practicing, Karin wanted to say, but couldn't, of course. She hated the smirks on their faces, hated the fact that she wasn't telling them the truth, hated that there was a "truth" to the whole charade.

"Karin was just buffing off some of my rough edges," Jed said, putting an arm around her waist.

She felt herself wilt into those rock-hard muscles of

his and hated every second of her helplessness. Fortunately, it was a temporary phenomenon. By Sunday night the cowboy would be gone and she would go back to being alone and strong. But tonight—

"We came to dance too," she announced. "So let's get in there and start having fun."

Well, they got in there, but Karin wasn't sure exactly when she was going to start having fun. It had been years since she had square-danced, and then it had only been a few times. She couldn't remember dosado from promenade, and swing from allemande.

Jed was patient, but she got worse with each set instead of better. She sashayed in when she should have sashayed out. Her courtesy turn got turned inside out. And her California twirl landed her in south New Jersey.

"Maybe I'll sit out this next set," she suggested when an interminable set ended.

"Good idea," he said. "We can find us a table over—"

"Oh, no. I just meant me. I'm not going to spoil your fun just because I'm rusty." She looked around and spotted a partnerless woman. "Nancy, Jed needs a partner for the next set. Can you take care of him?"

"Karin, really—"

But Nancy was ready, willing and able. "Dance with a real cowboy? You betcha."

"Great." Karin left the two together and joined Dorothy and Toto at a table overlooking the dance floor.

"Decided not to try one of the harder ones?" Dorothy asked.

"Harder ones?" Karin said as she sat down, her eyes on Nancy and Jed. There was a sudden sour feeling in her stomach.

"Yeah. They said the calls would be advanced," Toto said. "We decided we weren't ready to risk public humiliation."

"Ah." That was something Nancy and Jed sure didn't have to worry about. They danced well together. As though they'd been doing it for years. Or should have been doing it for years. Or were meant to do it. Karin sighed, annoyed with herself and them.

"Good crowd here tonight," she said brightly as she looked everywhere but at Jed.

"Wow, Jed sure is good," Dorothy said.

"Of course, I never come, so maybe this is the regular number of people," Karin went on, watching another group of couples come in through the main door.

"My feet couldn't move that fast on a dance floor," Toto said.

Karin turned back toward Jed, not by choice, but somehow feeling drawn to watch him. She spotted him easily, though his wasn't the only light-colored cowboy hat in the hall. Her eyes just seemed to know where he was all the time. Scary.

The caller was shouting out something about an Alamo swing-through, and she let herself relax and enjoy watching the dance. Jed was good. He moved so quickly, so easily, so—

Suddenly his knee seemed to give out and he collapsed.

Chapter Seven

"I'm fine," Jed said and got awkwardly to his feet. Everybody was staring at him—but with horror on their faces not admiration. He hobbled over a few feet to pick up his hat. His knee hurt like hell, but there was no reason to mention that. "This is nothing. I've hurt lots worse in my time."

Karin put his arm over her shoulder. "You aren't fine," she pointed out. "You can hardly walk. We need to take you to the doctor."

"Want us to call an ambulance?" Heather asked, hovering close also.

"Toto's got his police car here," Dorothy said. "He can run you over to the emergency room faster."

An emergency room? What kind of man interrupted a lady's night out for a trip to an emergency room—because he was injured *dancing*? Karin had really wanted to go square dancing tonight and he was not going to let her miss a minute of it.

He put his hat back on his head and turned slightly so that she wasn't supporting him, but was in his embrace. "You're all the doctor I need, darlin'."

Heather and Dorothy groaned, but Karin turned a delightful shade of pink. Her eyes looked a bit stormier, so he tried hard not to look at them.

"I specialize in cardiac surgery," she said. "Not orthopedics." Her voice was stiff with the embarrassment he'd come to expect with each public display of affection.

"And it's my heart that needs mending," he assured her, taking her hand and putting it over his racing heart. "I only tripped because you were frowning at me."

The others laughed, but Karin didn't seem to know how to react. She pulled away her hand. "I wasn't frowning at you."

"Prove it then." He took her hand back. "Come on, darlin', they're starting another set."

She did frown at him then. "You can't be thinking of dancing some more," she cried. "If you won't let us take you to the emergency room, I'm taking you home."

He supposed going home was best, but he hated to ruin her evening. "We don't have to go," he said. "How about if I sit down and you and your friends can stay and dance?"

Dorothy laughed. "Jed, if I didn't know Karin better, I'd think she tripped you just to have an excuse to leave. She was ready to go home when you got here."

He turned to look at Karin. The blush on her cheeks was proof enough that Dorothy's words were true. So why had they come?

"Okay, darlin'," he said and slipped his arm around her shoulders. "You can take me home for some TLC."

The blush deepened and he could feel her wanting to pull away, but she walked with him to the Jeep, their friends close behind. Jed wasn't sure if they were waiting for the next lip-to-lip show to begin or were afraid he was going to collapse. Either way, he wasn't going to entertain them. He pulled the car keys from his jeans' pocket.

"Oh no you don't." Karin took the keys from his hand. "I'm driving."

"I'm fine."

"Great. I'm still driving."

With a sigh, he limped over to the passenger side and climbed in. He gritted his teeth a bit, but it was probably too dark for anyone to have noticed.

"I'll follow along behind, in case you need help getting him up to the apartment," Toto said.

"Good idea," Dorothy agreed.

Except that he didn't need a nursemaid. "I'm fine," Jed said again.

No one paid any attention. Karin just started up the car.

"So why did we come if you hate square dancing?" he asked as they pulled from the church lot.

"Who says I hate square dancing?"

"Dorothy did." Damn knee. All he had to do was look at it and it got sprained. He winced as they went over a pothole.

"I'm sorry," Karin cried. "I didn't see it."

"I'm fine," he assured her. "Except for this curiosity that's eating away at me. Probably at my kneecap, too."

She slowed down to turn a corner, then glanced his way. It was too dark to see her expression, but he could feel hesitation about her.

"I wanted you to have an evening that you'd enjoy," she said.

Where had she gotten the idea that he'd enjoy square dancing? But there was too much vulnerability in her voice to point out that he hated it.

"That was sure nice of you," he said slowly.

He could feel her smile. "You've been so great about all this, I thought it would pay you back a little," she went on.

Lordy, he thought and tried to shift his position, but he couldn't find a spot where his knee—or heart— didn't ache. Good thing this was just make-believe. Otherwise he'd have to take up square dancing just to keep her feelings from getting hurt.

"You didn't have to," he said.

"I sure didn't think this would happen," she said, the smile gone from her voice. "I should have realized you'd be tired from working on the brick-painting crew today and planned something quieter."

Quieter? He wasn't an old man that ran out of energy when the sun went down. "Painting had nothing to do with anything," he said. "I've just got a bum knee from bull riding. And this was the nicest thing anybody's done for me in a long while."

"Really?"

Her voice sounded as if she was blushing as she pulled into the lot behind the bar. He was tempted to see if blushing made her lips hotter.

His heart began to beat a little faster as he became aware of her nearness. He'd hardly have to move to touch her, to pull her into his arms. Once she stopped the car, she'd turn toward him and he could—

The sound of another car pulling into the lot reminded him that Toto had come along. Damn. No, it was just as well. But not because he needed any help. Jed opened the car door.

Karin wasn't pleased with his show of independence. "Wait until—"

"I'm fine, darlin'." Too fine. Too tempted was more like it. He needed to get out of the inviting darkness of the car and into the bright lights of the apartment where he could breathe again. He slid out of the car and limped toward the stairs with a wave at Toto. "Thanks, but I'm fine."

"Are you sure?" Toto got out of his car, but Jed just waved again and made his way over to the stairs.

"Will you wait a minute?" Karin muttered as she caught up with him. "Let me take your arm."

"Actually, I think it's best if I use the handrails," he said. "You get too close and I get distracted."

"Oh, don't be silly," she said. "No one's here to see you."

That was the scary part. But rather than think about it, he began to pull himself up the stairs.

"Need any help?" Toto asked from the bottom of the stairs.

"No, thanks anyway," Jed said without turning. Karin was right behind him and he didn't need to be reminded of her presence.

Hell. What was he thinking? He didn't need to see her to know she was there. He went slowly up the steps as Toto got back in his car. A moment later, Jed heard it pull from the lot. He was relieved that Karin's friend had left, but wasn't sure he liked being alone with her again.

The porch got brighter suddenly as the kitchen door opened and Marge came outside. "Heavens, what happened?" she asked. "Jed, why are you limping?"

Lissa appeared in the doorway. "What's wrong?"

"I hurt my leg," Jed said, climbing up the last step. "A little."

Lissa came closer. "It wasn't your right knee, was it?"

"As a matter of fact, it was," Karin said.

"Oh, great." The girl rolled her eyes. "He's had that knee reconstructed like three times already. Did he tear any ligaments?"

Karin gave Jed a glare that seared the tips of his ears. "I don't know," she told Lissa. "He wouldn't let us take him to a doctor."

"That's just like him," Lissa said.

"It's only a sprain," Jed pointed out sharply. "And maybe a pulled muscle. I'll be fine in a day or two."

"Good gracious, get in here and sit down," Marge said, holding open the kitchen door. "Do you need an ice pack or anything?"

"No, I'm fine." How many times had he said that in the last half hour? Maybe he needed to get it tattooed on his forehead.

He went into the apartment, ignoring Lissa's scolding glare and Karin's hovering. Heck, he hardly limped at all and certainly didn't wince each time he put weight on the protesting joint.

"I bet it isn't even sprained," he said.

"Actually, an ice pack sounds like a good idea." Karin closed the kitchen door and frowned at Jed. "Sit down. I'm going to take a look at your knee."

He didn't like the fire in her eye. "I'm okay standing."

"You're right," she said.

She'd agreed too easily. He had the uneasy feeling he should have sat when he had the chance.

"You might as well go on into the bedroom," she said. "Can you strip off your jeans yourself or will you need my help?"

Toto went back to the VFW hall. He wasn't sure why. He wasn't keen on square dancing. But he was keen on one of the square dancers, he admitted to himself, and he wasn't going to miss a chance to see her. Pretty pitiful.

Dorothy, Heather and Alex were waiting for him in the lobby. His heart skipped a beat, but he knew he was being foolish. And Dorothy's words confirmed it.

"How was he?" she asked as soon as he came in.

"Okay, I guess," Toto said, feeling like a selfish jerk for even half wishing Dorothy's first thoughts had been of him. No wonder she didn't love him, not with the kind of attitude he had.

"He seemed to be moving okay while he was here," Alex said.

Toto nodded. "I would guess it hurt from the way he was limping, but he went up the stairs by himself. Took him a while though."

"Didn't you help him up?" Heather asked.

"He didn't want my help," Toto pointed out.

"You should have helped him anyway," Dorothy insisted.

He sighed. "There're times when a man's got nothing left but his pride. You don't take that away from him."

"What's pride got to do with anything?" Dorothy snapped and turned to the others. "Come on, guys. You gonna dance some more?"

Her voice was icy with annoyance and Toto just kept silent. So much for impressing her, for sweeping her off her feet with his heroics.

Heather went with Dorothy into the hall but Alex stayed behind. His smile was sympathetic.

"You couldn't have done it any other way," he said.

"That's not what Dorothy thinks. Maybe guys in Paris do things differently."

"I doubt it. Dorothy's still looking for that knight in shining armor that's going to carry her off."

"Yeah, but she'd clobber him first for not asking permission."

"I'm not sure this is a good idea," Jed said.

Karin just frowned at his knee, trying to ignore the rest of his body. He was sitting on the edge of her bed, wearing a perfectly respectable pair of boxer shorts. A shirt covered his chest. There was no reason for her to feel self-conscious. She was a doctor, after all. She had seen lots of naked men before. And Jed wasn't even naked, so what was the big deal?

She took a deep breath and bent down to gingerly touch his injured knee. It would really help if she knew what she was looking for. Besides trouble, that is.

She pressed gently on the side of the knee, ignoring the fluttery twinge in her belly, the curling tightening whisper of desire. "Does that hurt?" she asked.

"No," he said.

She felt the other side, willing that uneasiness in her stomach to go away. "How about this?"

"Nope." He swung his lower leg out slightly, then

rubbed just above his knee. "It's a little sore up here and aches a bit around the sides when I walk. Only a sprain."

She should take his word for it. That would be the smart thing to do. Just take his word for it and back off. Instead, she traced her finger gently along a thin scar that ran down the middle of his knee. It started a tingle up and down her spine and left her feeling almost limp.

"This from one of your knee surgeries?" she asked.

"Actually from more than one," he said. "They did a couple in the same spot."

"Both from rodeo injuries?"

"Both from getting tossed by the same bull," he said. "Guess you could say I was a slow learner."

Karin let her finger glide over to another scar on the side of his leg, the tingle along her back began to spread to other parts of her. Maybe she was a slow learner too. She knew this wasn't the smartest thing to be doing but...

"How'd you get this scar?" It was too jagged to be from surgery.

"Got tossed onto a fence."

"By the same bull?"

"His cousin."

She winced at the battering his body had taken. "Why did you keep going back? Are you that stubborn?"

"The money was good."

What a crazy answer. A typical macho-cowboy response. "So you'd save enough for your ranch and be too crippled up to enjoy it," she snapped. "Now that's real logic."

"Hey, I didn't get hurt that much," he protested.

"Oh, no? What about this scar and this one here? Or this—"

She'd been about to touch one higher up on his leg, but he took hold of her hand and stopped her. "I really don't think this is a good idea."

Suddenly the tingle came back in full force, a galloping shiver that raced through her and set every nerve on edge. Left every part of her aching in awareness of him. Her heart was beating so hard and fast that she could barely think.

She got to her feet slowly, her eyes locked with his. This was crazy. She was a doctor and he was hurt. There wasn't anything else going on. There shouldn't be anything else. So why were her lips longing to feel his? Why did her hands want to explore the hardness of his muscles? Why did she know that paradise was to be found in his arms?

The twinge in her belly came again, but this time it was different. It was definite. Not a sensual response but something else. Bubbles.

Her expression must have changed, for Jed frowned.

"What's the matter?" he asked as he stood up.

She shook her head, her hand going to her stomach as if that would make a difference. Maybe it was something she ate. Or maybe the dancing had been too much for her.

"Are you okay?" he asked, sounding more concerned.

"I'm fine," she said. "Just a little flutter in my stomach."

That didn't seem to ease his concern. "Maybe you should sit down."

"I don't feel faint." She shouldn't have said anything. She hated being fussed over. "Just flutter. Like I have bubbles bursting."

He got an odd look in his eyes and put his hand on her belly. The odd look turned to a smile. "Your baby's moving," he cried and moved her hand to where his had been.

She felt slight movement, both from inside and outside, and took her hand away as if that would make it stop. "It's too early for that."

"No, it's not." He put his hand there again, a soft smile lighting his eyes. "Isn't that the most marvelous thing?"

What? To have a baby that would have no father and a mother that didn't know how to love? But she couldn't say any of that to him.

"You should stay off that leg," she said instead and took a step back.

Something seemed to close down in his eyes as he looked at her, then he slowly nodded. "Right," he said. "I'm sorry. This isn't something you'd be wanting to share with me, is it?"

It wasn't him. It wasn't as if there was somebody else. It was just—

She sighed and went to the bedroom door. "I'm going to get you an ice pack so you can ice that knee before you go to sleep."

Jed spent the night brooding about how he hated being sick. Hated being injured. Hated being waited on. He knew he would have to stay off his knee for it to heal, but he hoped he'd be able to see to it alone. Lissa was off at school again and Karin had better things to do than hang around the apartment and watch him.

Of course there also was the fact that he was finding her too damn attractive. A little distance between them wouldn't be a bad thing.

"You know, I'm really fine on my own," he told her after breakfast the next morning. "I'll just settle down with the newspaper."

"I don't have anywhere I need to go," she said as she started for her bedroom, then stopped. "Do you have any laundry you want me to do? I don't think I have a full load with just my stuff."

He ignored her question. "Shouldn't you be checking on your patients?" he asked. "What about that guy you operated on on Monday?"

"My partner is taking care of him."

"Oh."

She went into her room and came out with an armload of clothes. Maybe she was taking them to a Laundromat. Or maybe she was washing each thing by hand and it would take her hours. He could always hope.

She carried the clothes into the next room and, after a little bit of thumping around, was back and settling down at the kitchen table with some medical journals. Two minutes, tops. If getting laundry started was a rodeo event, she'd be the champ. Why did Marge have to supervise yellow-brick painting all morning? But that did give him an idea.

"Maybe we should go downstairs and get the bar ready to open for your mother. Her festival work this morning is going to set her back."

Karin barely looked up from her journals. "I have no idea what she does to get the place ready to open. We'd probably screw up more than we'd help."

But at least he wouldn't be sitting here watching her, having his blood turn to fire with every move she made.

Of course, he didn't have to sit here. He could go into the living room.

"I'm going to sit in the living room," he said and picked up his newspaper. "I can stretch my leg out there."

"What? Oh, the living room."

She'd only been reading for a few moments, but she had been engrossed in the article already. There was something lost and vulnerable about her as she looked up at him. It tore at him for some unknown reason and he had to fight back the urge to brush that hair away from her face. To touch that—

"I could come in there and read too," she said, starting to stand up.

"No! Uh…I mean, I'm afraid I'd disturb you," he said quickly. "I…uh…like to watch game shows on TV while I'm reading the paper and I'm sure you'd prefer it to be quiet."

"Well, I'll help you get settled," she offered and did get to her feet this time. She took the newspapers from him and offered him her arm.

He could hardly refuse, so he made himself limp into the other room as fast as possible and practically jumped onto the sofa. He barely noticed how soft and sweet her perfume was, or how smooth her skin was. Or—

He swallowed hard. "This is great. Thanks," he said.

She put the newspapers on the low table in front of the sofa, then frowned at him. "Would you like a soda? Or some more coffee?"

"Nope, I'm just fine." He picked up the sports section of the paper, hopefully showing how eager he was to read it.

"Oh, I know," she murmured and flicked on the TV before bringing him the remote. "Don't want you to miss those game shows."

He stared at the cheerful TV host and his perky guests and wondered what the hell show this was. He sure hoped Karin didn't ask any questions.

He smiled up at her. "Thanks."

This time he did bury his head in the newspaper and kept it there until he heard the sound of her kitchen chair being pulled out. Then he breathed a sigh of relief. Marge's cat was crawling into his lap at that moment and gave him a strange look.

"Okay, so this is harder than I thought," he muttered to Shilah. "It's not like I've done this before, you know."

"What did you say?" Karin called to him from the kitchen.

"Nothing," Jed assured her. "Just answering a question on the TV. If I get too loud, I won't mind if you go into the bedroom to read. Or even downstairs to the bar."

She laughed. "The noise won't bother me at all. And I'd rather stay where I can see you. I'm not convinced you won't try something if I don't keep an eye on you."

"All I'm going to do is try to guess the answer to this puzzle," he said, nodding at the television.

"Oh."

With a sigh, Jed went back to the newspaper. The morning passed with all the speed of a pickup without wheels. He read every danged article in the newspaper—twice. He petted Shilah until she finally went off to the other side of the room to get away from him. And he watched game shows until he was ready to throw something at the next cheery face he saw. He still was conscious of every move Karin made. Every sigh, every stretch, every shift of her position. And the fire inside him grew.

He tried to nap; it didn't work. He tried to turn his back to her; he could see the reflection of her silhouette in the TV and the windows. He tried to close his eyes and pretend he was back home; his imagination worked overtime with every sound in the apartment and Karin was somehow the star.

Instead of thinking about Karin, he decided to think about lunch. Maybe they would go out and get something to eat. Someplace where there were lots and lots of people. He'd like a hamburger, smothered in onions and cheese and mushrooms. Or they could get a pizza, a deep-dish with green peppers and pepperoni. And didn't someone mention a great place in town for barbecue chicken?

"Oh, gosh. Look at the time," Karin muttered in the kitchen. "I'd better get started on lunch."

"Why don't we go out?" he suggested.

She stopped in the doorway to frown at him. "You need to stay off that knee, remember?"

"Then why don't we order in?" Maybe they could convince the delivery person to stay and eat with them.

"Don't be silly," she said. "Mom's got lots of food here. I can throw something together."

But before she had a chance, the doorbell rang and Dorothy came in with pizza. Jed had never been so glad to see anyone in his life. He limped into the kitchen.

"How's the knee?" Dorothy asked.

"Great. Fine," he said.

"It looked like you were limping," she said with a frown.

"He was," Karin pointed out. "He's supposed to stay off it."

"I had to come out here to eat," he said. And to look for the sanity he was rapidly losing.

"I could have brought the pizza in there," Dorothy said. "Or just dropped it off for you two to share. I don't need to stay and eat with you."

"No, stay," he said quickly. Too quickly, he guessed since he got decidedly odd looks from Karin and Dorothy. "Uh, Karin's going stir-crazy cooped up here with me."

Dorothy burst out laughing. "What? You two can't think of anything to do that would keep Jed off his feet?"

"Dorothy!" Karin protested, her cheeks a fiery red.

This wasn't much help. He went to the refrigerator to pour glasses of lemonade. "So, Dorothy, tell us all about Paris."

"Oh, heavens, what's to tell?" she said and brought the glasses over that he'd poured. "I'd much rather hear what it's like being a cowboy." Dorothy paused and looked at Karin, a gleam in her eyes. "Or being engaged to one."

"Golly, that's all anybody wants to talk about since we got here," Karin said. "I'd love to hear what it's like to live in Paris."

Dorothy shook her head. "That's all anybody wants to talk about."

"I've got a great idea then," Jed said. "Why don't we eat?"

They had a great lunch, with lots of chatter about nothing, but it didn't take up nearly enough time. Before he knew it, the pizza was long gone, the lemonade all drunk and Dorothy was leaving. The torture of being alone with Karin would begin all over again. Unless he could do something about it.

"I'll clean up," he told Karin as she walked Dorothy to the door. "You want to go out with Dorothy, go ahead. I'll be fine."

"No." She turned and gave him a frown that would have slowed a lesser man. "Get back on the sofa and rest that leg."

He gave her a winning smile. "Look, I'm just going to wash a few dishes and, nimble though I am, I don't do that with my feet."

"I think this is where I should leave," Dorothy said. "Bye all."

The door was barely closed behind her when Karin had his arm in a monster grip. "Will you get back to the sofa and sit down?"

"I can't just lie around all day."

"Yes, you can," she said.

"No, I can't," he insisted. "I'm not made to sit still that long."

"Then I'll help you." Karin pulled him toward the living room.

"I can walk, you know."

"Then walk over to that sofa and sit down."

But with her so close to him, with her scent filling up his air and her softness calling to him, his feet didn't seem to work. Hers didn't seem to either, and they just stood there for a long moment, staring into each other's eyes.

Then ever so slowly, he put his hand on her back, pulled her to him and gave her a light kiss. Just a little one, nothing serious.

And he had every intention of stopping right there. That little kiss would be enough to take the edge off his desire. It would be enough to warn them both of the dangers of dancing across quicksand. But there was something in her eyes that drew him.

He put his arms around her and drew her close. Very close. So close that air couldn't have squeezed through the space between them. And this time he was damn serious about it.

He brought his lips down to meet hers, needing to savor their softness, their warmth, their wondrous power. But only for a moment. It would be a quick glimpse of the sun, a quick taste of sweetness, a quick touch of velvet.

Her lips were like golden honey though, and he could not pull away. Their taste, their touch, their potent magic wove a spell all through him of wonder and desire. He wondered how he had lived without her sustenance. The merest touch and he needed her with a power that stunned him, that drove his body hot and hard.

He kissed her again, his mouth pressed to hers with an urgency that took him by storm. His hands held her close, her softness pressed against him. There was a fire raging inside him. Her touch had been a lightning strike that ignited the kindling of his heart. He tried to put it out, but it was a prairie fire burning out of control.

His hands roamed over her back, trying to mold her to fit his need, and every place he touched only made the fire stronger, the desire hotter. He could scarcely breathe or think, but he could feel and want and need and touch. This was heaven and all of paradise awaited, if only—

He pulled away from her, a breath of sanity coming at last, though it was pitifully meager. His legs felt as wobbly as his good sense and Karin looked more than a tad shaky herself.

"You really have to rest," she said.

Jed didn't say anything as he limped the few feet to the sofa. A cold shower would be more effective. He stared at the television, trying to keep his eyes away from Karin.

"And I have to figure out what to make for dinner," Karin said.

Dinner? That was good. Jed tried to concentrate on an ad for macaroni. Food would cool his desire; he just had to think food thoughts. "Cook up some hot dogs," he suggested.

"No." Karin frowned. "You don't feed junk food to a child for dinner."

Somehow his gaze had crept back to her, and her worried frown tugged at his heart. He wanted to kiss it away. He wanted to take her lip, that pouty lower one, and pull at it gently with his teeth. He wanted to pull at it with his mouth and lick its softness with his tongue. He wanted to—

He needed to get ahold of himself. "Why don't I spring for dinner?" he suggested.

"You can't do that."

"Sure I can." It was perfect. He owed Karin big time anyway for all she was trying to do for him. Dinner out would be a start. "All I need is my wallet. That kind of springing has nothing to do with my legs."

Karin didn't say anything.

Besides, if he stayed here this evening, alone with her and his desires, he'd regret it in the morning. They both would and he was not into making regrets. "I'm a fast healer."

She grunted.

"But only if I have an incentive."

She looked at him and the air suddenly vanished. Breathing was as impossible as thinking. The hunger was back, the desperate driving need. He felt as if they were teetering on the edge of a cliff. One false move, one more heated look, and they'd tumble over.

He forced himself to look away. "Dinner at one of Chesterton's best restaurants," he said quickly. "That would be a powerful incentive."

"All right."

He felt her move and he found that he could breathe again.

"We'll see how you are later," she said. "If you're up to going out, we will. Otherwise we'll order in."

"Deal." He leaned back and closed his eyes in relief. He'd battled his desires and won. This time.

But there was no way in hell they were going to stay here this evening. All he had to do was walk without a limp and he didn't see that that would be a problem. Hell, he'd walked on a broken leg in his time.

Maybe they'd even do something after dinner, just the two of them since Lissa was working on her costume at Ginger's house again. Nothing risky like dancing or sipping wine by candlelight. No, something safe, but something that Karin would enjoy. Something that would show his gratitude for today.

And he thought he saw an ad in the newspaper for the perfect thing.

No matter how obviously Jed tried to hide his limp, Karin had been prepared to pretend she was fooled.

After spending all day cooped up with him in that tiny apartment, she needed to be around other people and get her common sense back. Her hormones had been working overtime and she needed to remind the little devils that she and Jed were not an item.

But by late afternoon, he was barely limping and Karin didn't have to pretend. They went to the Landing for a leisurely dinner that went by far too quickly. Since when was service so fast, and elaborate dinners so easy to prepare? Her only hope was that her mother had closed the bar early and was up in the apartment. No chance of that.

"You know, you two could go out someplace after you drop me off at Ginger's," Lissa said as they finished dinner.

"That would be nice," Karin said, hoping she didn't sound too eager.

"Good, because I had something planned." Jed paid the bill and they got to their feet.

"A movie?" Lissa asked as they left the restaurant. "What're you gonna go see?"

"We're going to see you off to Ginger's," Jed said.

Lissa had a half pout on her face but skipped along with them. "You're coming to the show at school tomorrow, aren't you both? Karin, you remind Daddy, okay? And make sure he knows where the school is."

"I'll do my best," Karin promised with a laugh, but a shadow fell across her evening.

It was so sweet, the rapport between Jed and Lissa. The way the little girl tried to take care of him while he was taking care of her. The obvious love they had for each other. She felt the fluttery feeling again and lightly placed her hand over her stomach. She wished she could promise her child that they'd have a wonderful life, just the two of them. But how could she? She had no idea how to parent, how to comfort away disappointments, how to soothe hurts and wipe away the pain, not just the tears.

She got into the Jeep and drove to Ginger's house, listening to Jed and Lissa talk. Even their normal everyday chatter was hard to listen to, hard not to feel the sting of fear nipping at her heels. Could she even do that with her child?

By the time they dropped Lissa off at Ginger's, Karin was exhausted. She was too tired to be in any danger from Jed's kisses. "I'm pretty worn out," she told Jed. "I'd just fall asleep in the theater and miss the movie."

"Lucky we aren't going to the movies then." He flashed her one of his big cowboy smiles. "Turn left up here and then right at the light."

"Where are we going?" She wasn't in the mood for a surprise.

"You'll see."

She sighed. But before she could tell him to quit playing games, he directed her into a big strip mall, filled with the usual assortment of large and small stores. And, judging from the banners and balloons, one of them was having a big promotion.

"I figured you work all the time," he said. "So we're going to do some browsing and fact-finding."

"Browsing? For what?" Oh, damn. Her stomach fell into her shoes. The store with the balloons and banners was a baby store. Panic clutched her throat in a death grip. "We don't have to do this tonight. I'm going to go to a baby-supply store in Chicago."

"Yeah, but they're having a baby fair. All sorts of

displays and product information. It'll give you a place to start from when you do the serious shopping.''

Karin could feel the Jeep's walls closing in on her. She should just drive back out of the lot, but if she did that, he'd want to know why.

"Why don't we go to a movie?" she suggested.

"We'll just go in and look around. After a few minutes, if you still want to go to a movie, we will.''

She pulled the Jeep into a parking spot. It would be okay. She would follow along with him, take a quick run through the store and then leave. They'd be out in fifteen minutes, twenty max. It wouldn't be hard.

Even with her pep talk, she almost bolted when they stepped inside the store. It wasn't the sappy music or all the blue and pink balloons or the miles of ribbon dangling from the ceiling. It was the millions of glowing pregnant woman, each one accompanied by a beaming husband.

"Hi, folks," a chipper, nonpregnant woman said, thrusting a little bunny rattle into Karin's hand. "Welcome to the Bunny's Hutch Baby Warehouse. Want to enter our drawing?"

Karin looked at the little plastic rattle in her hand as if it were a poisonous spider and shrank back into Jed's body. His arm went around her, but it brought no comfort.

"First prize is a completely furnished nursery," the woman went on.

Karin looked up then, her hand tightening around the rattle as if that would somehow close off its power. "No, no. I don't live here.''

"You can use your mother's address," Jed pointed out.

"Yes," the woman agreed. "That would—"

"I said no," Karin cried out and hurried down the nearest aisle.

Right into a woman demonstrating various models of mobiles.

Karin pretended to give them a glance and tried to hurry along, but Jed made her stop. He wanted her to look at the mobile with smiling dinosaurs and listen to the music on the one with smiling suns. She felt the horror rising in her with each second she was at the display. Each time that horrible mobile swung around and those awful suns grinned at her.

"Yes, they're great, but I...I...I already have one," she lied. "A friend from work gave me one. It's really cute."

"Oh, okay," Jed said and finally let her move on, only to stop her at the display of cribs.

There were eight different models there, in different colors and styles. Early American. French provincial. One with a ruffly canopy. She just stared at them, her breath coming in short gasps. They were so solid and definite and...and...and once she had one she couldn't try to pretend this wasn't all happening. But what if she bought the wrong kind? What if her baby hated French provincial?

"This is a good brand," Jed was saying as they looked at a plain white model. "And it's got teething rails."

Teething rails? What in the world were teething rails? What if she got a crib without them? She swallowed the fear that seemed ready to choke her and moved into the next aisle.

It was filled with little gadgets—bouncing things you hung in doorways, walkers and wind-up swings. Not to mention enough clothes to outfit every Third World child on the planet. All things that her baby would need, and along with them, Karin would need to know when to use them. How to use them. If to use them.

She felt sick to her stomach. She should never have eaten dinner, and wouldn't have if she'd had any idea Jed was planning this.

"Oh, these are great." Jed stopped in front of a display of pouches for carrying a baby.

The woman running the display came over with a smile. "These are for newborns and we have models for children on up to twenty-five pounds." She was wearing a cocoonlike canvas sack with a doll in it and patted it as she spoke.

Karin stared at it, trying to will her stomach to settle and her breath to slow. This carrier was okay. It was simple. She could handle this.

"This is the greatest invention since sliced bread," the woman was going on. "It's easy on your back and puts the child where you can always see it. But, even more important, the baby can always see you."

Other couples—real couples, Karin thought—had come over to see the display and the woman spun back and forth in a half-circle motion to let everyone see how the baby pouch fit.

"You can be shopping, making dinner or watching TV," she went on. "No matter what you're doing, your baby will be able to look up at you and see your love for him or her."

Her love? The words cut into Karin like a knife.

"How sweet," someone was murmuring.

"I love it," someone else agreed.

But what if there was no love in her face? Karin wanted to ask—wanted to scream. *What if the baby could tell its mother had no heart?*

The store was closing in on her. The happiness of the couples there was smothering her, cutting off all the air, and there was only one thing Karin could do.

She turned and ran down the aisle toward the exit.

She heard Jed calling her, but she didn't stop. She couldn't. She had to get out of here. Away from all the happy couples and the good parents and the people so filled with love that their children would be content and successful and never know a moment's anguish.

All she could do was run down the aisle, shouldering aside the couples in the way, and then out into the darkness of the parking lot.

The good news was, she'd parked the Jeep close to the entrance and had no trouble finding it, even with tears blinding her. The bad news was, she couldn't seem to open the door, so she just lay against it and cried.

Chapter Eight

Jed was more than concerned. He was terrified. What in the world was going on? But he didn't ask, just got the car keys from Karin and helped her into the car. Why the hell hadn't he paid attention when she'd said she didn't want to go in there? Obviously she was still trying to come to terms with the pregnancy and abandonment.

"I'm really sorry." He drove from the parking lot. "I just thought—"

"No, I'm the one that should be apologizing," she said, her voice none too steady, but the tears had stopped. "I acted like an idiot. I really do need to start getting stuff for the baby."

"But it didn't have to be tonight," he said.

"It's not like waiting is going to change anything."

"You never know."

She went silent then, turning to stare out the window

at the passing night. Whatever Karin needed to bring her good spirits back, Jed would provide it. He'd sit and listen, he'd bake cookies, he'd sing her cowboy songs. Anything. If she needed it, he'd do it.

He pulled into the parking lot behind the bar, thankful that Marge would still be down in the bar for another several hours. If Karin wanted to talk, she could. Or she could cry some more, or they could watch TV and pretend that nothing had happened.

"I vote we go upstairs, kick off our shoes and take a few deep breaths. And then, if you want to talk, I'm here."

She nodded slowly, so he got out and went around to open the passenger-side door. She was frowning at him when he got there.

"I should have been driving," she said. "I forgot all about your leg."

"My leg is fine," he said as he took her arm. "I only let you drive earlier because I was being nice."

That won him a slight smile though it had faded away by the time they got into the kitchen. He'd make sure the next one lasted longer.

"Why don't you go set yourself down, darlin'?" He tossed his hat onto the kitchen table. "I'll pour us something cool and satisfying."

Once Karin went into the living room, he poured them each a glass of lemonade and joined her. She was sitting on the sofa, her mother's cat curled up next to her. If it weren't for the shadows in her eyes, she would have looked relaxed and content.

"I took your advice about my shoes," she said, wiggling her toes.

"Good." He handed her a glass and then flopped

down on the sofa, kicking off his boots once he sat down. "That feels good."

She took a sip of lemonade and then looked away from him. "I really am sorry about tonight."

He sighed and leaned back on the sofa. "If you don't quit saying you're sorry, you're going to be in deep trouble."

She turned back toward him. "Oh, that sounds scary."

Jed looked into her big blue eyes. Not too many minutes ago they were wide and fearful-looking, like those of a mare trapped in a barbed wire fence. Now they were more steady, but there was an underlying ripple or two that said she was not really over whatever was troubling her.

"You better believe it's scary," he said, putting a hand on her shin. "Something really bad can happen if you say you're sorry one more time."

"Like what?"

She didn't exactly have a smile on her lips, but there was a little more lightness in her voice. His own spirits rose. "Oh, I might do something really drastic." He looked down at the beautiful leg that his hand was rubbing. "Like maybe tickle your feet."

"I wouldn't advise that."

"Why not?"

"Because then I'd have to kill you. Slowly and painfully."

"Hmm," he said, running his hand up and down her leg.

"I'd do the slow part, you'd get the pain."

"Double hmm." He pulled her feet onto his lap. "Your words certainly give a man reason to ponder."

"I hope that means you're not going to do something dumb."

Her tone was weary but she left her feet where they were. He felt her tense up a tad.

"All I can promise is I'll seriously ponder things," he said, setting his hands to rubbing her legs, starting from her calves and working down to her ankles. "Anything else we have to leave to chance."

"I hope you realize that if Chance does something I don't like, you're the one whose health is going to suffer."

Jed could feel the stiffness melt out of her leg muscles and could see gentle clouds roll into the deep blue sky of her eyes. "My daddy told me that life was hazardous to a man's health."

Karin looked at him but then shut her eyes as she lay back. It was several moments before she spoke again. "I really think you should stop that."

"Why?"

"Because it feels good. Too good."

Jed let his hands go down to her feet, gently massaging first one and then the other. He could almost see her tension spilling out on the floor. "Mamas tend to get achy feet," he said. "Carrying a new baby puts a bigger load than normal on them."

"Aren't you going to stop?" she asked.

"Only if you really want me to."

"I told you it feels too good," she said, her words breathy.

"What's wrong with that?" he asked.

Her eyes slowly opened. "It's just a short hop from feeling good to hurting," she replied.

Jed was silent a long moment but he continued his

foot massage. "You sound like you've taken that trip before."

"Hasn't everybody?"

He guessed she was right, but there was just so much acceptance and resignation in her voice that he wanted to argue the point. Instead, he leaned over and kissed her mounded tummy.

"That's the first time my baby's been kissed."

"Is that so? Then we better make sure it's not the last." He bent forward to kiss her stomach again. When he looked up, tears were streaming down her face. He must have screwed up again. "I'm sorry. I just wanted to show the kid that it was coming into a world of love."

Suddenly her tears weren't silent. He pulled her into his arms. "What's the matter?" He gently kissed the top of her head. "What did I do now?"

"You didn't do anything," she said. "At least not anything bad."

"But you're upset."

"I'm upset because—" she couldn't seem to get the words out "—because I don't know if my baby is coming into a world of love. I don't know that I'll be able to give it the love it needs."

"That's ridiculous." He took his handkerchief out of his pocket and, lifting her head, gently dabbed at the tears. "Now, I know it's a little hard for you to kiss the tyke right now, but in your heart—"

"That's the whole problem," she snapped halfheartedly at him. "I told you before, I don't have a heart."

Jed shook his head. "Karin, darlin', everybody's scared before they have a baby, but it always works out just fine. Once you see that little tyke, you're gonna be filled with love for it."

Karin pulled away from him. "You don't understand. I've never been filled with love for anything."

He found himself frowning at her. "Oh, come on. You love your mother. It's obvious."

"That's different." She got to her feet. "Besides, is it love or just respect? I care for her certainly, but I'm not sure it's really love."

"Maybe you have to stop analyzing and let yourself feel," he said.

"That's just it," she cried. "I don't feel. What kind of a mother can I be if I don't feel anything?"

Karin was sorry she'd said the words as soon as they left her mouth. She was sure Jed would pull away and she'd see dislike and disgust in his eyes. But she didn't. There was only softness and sadness there, and a gentleness in his touch.

"If you don't feel anything, why are you so upset?" he asked.

"Because I'm scared," she said. How could he not understand?

"But isn't that feeling something? And if you didn't want the best for your baby, would you be scared?"

His words almost made sense, but she was too far down this road to be detoured. She walked over to the window and pulled the drape aside to look down at the street below. Soft circles of light broke free of the darkness and she could see a couple walking slowly along the street, hand in hand. But that would never be her. She was lost in the shadows.

Jed pulled the drape from her hand and let it fall back across the window. She looked at him, then turned slowly so that she was facing him. He was so kind, so understanding. She didn't feel cold and unloving with him. She didn't feel as though a wall had been built around her, keeping her from feeling anything.

She reached out and lightly touched the top button of his shirt. She couldn't quite meet his eyes. "When I was younger, I was proud that I didn't feel things," she told him, her voice low and unsteady. "But it doesn't feel so great now. It feels lonely."

His hand brushed her cheek with such softness it might have been a dream, but then he lifted her chin slightly so that her eyes met his. "It doesn't have to be," he said. "You just have to reach out and let someone hold you. Let someone be close to you."

She had tried that before with Rico and it hadn't worked. But it had been different. She had wanted to be in love with him, not just love him for a night. She had been looking for something mighty and lasting, something to write songs about, not just to be held when she was hurting. Would it be so bad to let Jed hold her? She didn't want anything else.

Rather than answer him, she leaned in close and let her lips touch his. She was whispering a question, asking for comfort, wondering if she could be held. Her mouth moved softly against his, her hurt fading slightly as other feelings grew. Ever so slowly, she slid her arms around his neck, only to discover she was in his arms also.

The kiss changed as their arms tightened around each other. Her touch stopped being tentative, a plea for the easing of her aches, and became seeking and driving. The hurt and loneliness were disappearing as this tightness, this hunger swept over her. She let her fingers run through his hair, let them roam over his back, let them feel the rock-hard muscles that allowed him to hold her so wonderfully tight.

He pulled his lips from hers and loosened his hold a bit as if gathering his wits. Or gathering some air. He took a deep breath, his eyes seeming to devour her. She could still feel the pressure of his lips on hers though the actual touch was gone.

"Maybe we'd better stop while we can," he said, his voice hoarse and low.

But the moments in his arms had been too wonderful. There had been no pain, no self-doubts, no fears. She didn't want to go back to her worries, not yet. She liked who she was in his embrace.

"Why?" she asked.

Her hold on him had loosened, too, but she slipped one hand down to lightly brush his cheek. She could feel a tremble rush through him and a shiver of answering desire washed over her.

"It's only for now," she said. "Only for tonight."

"You've been hurt enough," he said.

"So heal me," she whispered and closed in on his mouth again.

This time the kiss was wild and rough. A run through the storm, a daring of the winds to throw them down. It was lightning and thunder all crashing together and shaking the heavens. It was hot and heavy and hard. Two hungry souls in search of peace.

"This is crazy," Jed said, pulling back once more.

"Yes." But she couldn't pull back. She didn't want to.

"We shouldn't go any further."

"Why not?"

She leaned into him, lying against his chest. Beneath her cheek she could hear, feel, his heart racing and she closed her eyes.

"There is some magic in being held," she whispered. "It seems to chip away at my fears and makes me believe I can be strong."

"You're making this very hard for me," he said softly.

"It doesn't have to be." Still lying against him, she let one hand work at the buttons on his shirt. One undone, then another, then another. "I don't want to wake in the middle of the night and only remember my fears."

She slipped her hand into his shirt and felt the hair on his chest. She slid her hand over it, and ran her fingers through it. He quivered beneath her touch and his hold on her tightened, but she could feel his iron control. She stopped and pulled completely away.

"Because I'm pregnant, right?" What a fool she'd been to think he would find her desirable just because she needed to feel she was.

"Good Lord, no," he said and pulled her right back into his arms. "You are so damn beautiful it hurts to look at you, but you are also so damn vulnerable now. I don't want to hurt you."

"I just want to be held," she said. "Is that so much to ask?"

"Too much. Way too much. I can't just hold you and not make love to you. I can't breathe in your softness and feel your tenderness and not want to make you mine." He put his hand on her belly and rubbed it ever so gently. "You have to be very sure before you push me any further."

She put her hand over his. "I am. Make me feel beautiful."

With a groan, he let go of her only to sweep her up in his arms. His lips pressed against her as he carried her into the bedroom, kicking the door closed behind him. She kissed him back with a hunger that was growing and surging, her arms tightening around him.

Then suddenly she was lying on her bed and he was there next to her. With slow precision, he unbuttoned her blouse and pushed it off her shoulders. His mouth rained kisses on her shoulders as his hands undid her bra and loosened it from her heavy breasts. Then his mouth played with them, each in turn, sending shivers of wild desire all through her.

She'd never been loved like this, made to feel so desirable and wanted. Her whole body trembled under his touch, his hands and his lips wove such a spell over her that she felt she would never be the same. He was bringing her body alive.

Reaching down, she unbuttoned the rest of his shirt and pulled it off him. His shoulders felt so massive beneath her hands, so hard and strong and so able to protect. She slid her hands under his arms and around to his back.

He was made of iron, but her hands ran over the knots and lines of a scar and stopped. There was another on his arm, she realized, and she leaned closer to brush it with her lips.

"Poor Jed," she breathed. "You're all beat up."

"Not nearly, lovely lady, not nearly."

There was something in his voice that reached into the core of her being, something that shook her and made her needs all the greater. Something that made her feel dainty and beautiful and all the more desired.

She sat up, missing his touch for the brief moment, and pulled off her slacks and panty hose. Even as she sat on the edge of the bed, his hands were reaching for her, his lips were blazing little paths along her heated skin. She lay back down at his side.

''I think you're overdressed, sir,'' she told him with a smile, touching his lips with one finger.

He grabbed up the hand to kiss it, then kiss each fingertip, sucking on it before letting her go. ''I was just thinking of shucking off these jeans, ma'am.'' His drawl was slow, just like the movement of his hands.

But he seemed more interested in lingering in his caresses than in taking off his jeans. His hands roamed over her, sliding with tantalizing hesitation over every spot that was sensitive to his touch. Which seemed to be just about everywhere. Her body felt as if it was on fire, as if it was tied up in knots and about to burst free.

''Will you take off those jeans?'' she whispered, trying to work around to get them off herself, but he kept moving just out of her reach.

''In a minute,'' he said.

But then his hands found a new spot to caress, to tease, to torment, and she forgot about everything else. They moved over her belly and across her thighs, and then lower and closer and over the center of her heat. She gasped at the sensation and almost pulled away, the pleasure was so intense, but he wouldn't let her. There was nowhere to go, and no place she wanted to go, but closer to him.

Her body trembled with unspoken needs, and she clung to him, but he slipped suddenly from her grasp and pulled off his jeans and shorts. Then he lay at her side, pulling her onto him.

''I don't want to put pressure on the baby,'' he whispered.

His hands moved over and over her, all the while guiding her to come down on top of him. She felt exposed this way, and for a split second embarrassed, but the hard wonder of him inside her was too magical. It sent sparks all through her body and she could do nothing but move in a rhythm of pleasure and desire.

She braced herself against him, digging her hands into the hair on his chest as wave after wave of ecstasy washed over her. Her hands opened and closed, driven by hunger and fulfillment, even as his hands caressed and stroked and drove her hungers hotter and wilder.

Then there was a magical moment when all the fires raged up together, when the hunger exploded into a cascade of shooting stars and they were one. She clung and held and tried to press even closer together as his body merged with hers. Time stood still.

After another moment, breaths returned and the fires slowed. Still entwined, they rolled onto their sides. Arms, legs, souls, still wrapped around the other. She lay against his chest, he pressed gentle kisses into her hair.

"That was some bronco I just rode, cowboy," she whispered.

"Give him a little time and you might find he's got some fire left."

She just smiled and snuggled deeper into his arms. Her eyes closed and she knew her dreams would be sweet tonight.

Karin came out of the bedroom, hesitantly. Shyly. Jed had to turn away, pretending to concentrate on the frying pan before him. Just the sight of her brought pain to his heart. He was glad, though, that Lissa and Marge had already left, so he and Karin were alone.

"How about an omelet, darlin'?"

"Sure," Karin said, her voice soft. "Sounds great."

Jed swallowed hard. Last night had been a horrible

mistake. He'd taken advantage of her vulnerability and now he had to pay the piper.

"Best wait until you taste it," he murmured.

"Somehow I can't see anything you do coming out poorly."

How about his decision making? The heat climbed up his neck like mercury in the thermometer at hell's gate. He moved quickly toward the refrigerator and opened the door. "Onions and green peppers okay?"

"Sure. I trust you."

The heat in his neck climbed higher and got so hot that he could smell burning hair. Jed took the eggs, green pepper, a sweet onion and a chunk of cheddar cheese out of the refrigerator and dumped them on the counter. After pulling out a knife from the drawer, he began to vigorously cut up the pepper. If only he could chop his transgression into such bite-size pieces, then maybe he could figure out what to do about the mess—

"Ow!" Jed dropped the knife and grabbed at a dish towel to stem the blood suddenly gushing from his finger. "Damn it."

"What did you do?" Karin said, rushing over. "Let me see that."

"No, I'm all right."

He tried to spin away from Karin but he found himself in the corner the cabinets formed with the stove.

"Stop acting so macho," Karin said. "Mother keeps her knives very sharp and I want to make sure that you're not going to lose a finger."

"I didn't cut it that bad," he grumbled.

Actually, if he was going to chop anything off, it'd be another part of his body. His fingers never caused him any problems so major.

"Jed, quit fooling around. I want to see your hand."

The tone was sharp and no nonsense. It was the voice of an experienced physician. Someone who expected to be obeyed. Jed held out his hand to her. Karin took off the towel and looked critically at his finger.

"It's a long cut," she said. "But fortunately it's not too deep."

"I told you it was nothing."

Karin gave him a dismissive look. "Wash your hand," she said, pushing him toward the sink. "And I'll get some gauze and tape."

He wanted to tell her again that he was all right but he knew a stone wall when he saw one.

"And don't even think of picking up that knife again," she called over her shoulder. "I'll take care of breakfast after I get you fixed up."

Shoulders slumping, Jed turned on the water and soaped his hands. He really was all right. And once his finger was taped up, he'd be able to handle fixing breakfast without any problem. Certainly more easily than he could return things to normal between him and Karin. He watched the water roll off his hand and wished he was anywhere but here.

It was all right for him to comfort Karin. To hold her. To tell her what a fine woman she was. That's what a man did. What she didn't deserve was for him to use her for satisfying his own lust. He should have controlled his urges. There was no excuse for what he'd done.

"Okay," she said, suddenly appearing at his side. "Let's get that finger bandaged. Then I think I'd better make breakfast. But tell me, are you always this accident-prone?"

"What do you mean?" he asked. "I just cut myself a little."

"And banged your shoulder and your head, and sprained your knee," she pointed out as she applied gauze to his wound. "If I didn't know better, I'd think Chesterton was dangerous."

It was turning out to be much more so than he'd ever expected. "Maybe I'm allergic to the place," he suggested.

"Good thing you're leaving in a few days then."

"Yeah. Good thing."

They both fell silent as she taped up his finger. It was a good job, as good as any bandage job he'd had over his career, but it did nothing for the major ache in his heart.

Chapter Nine

"Okay," the photographer said, holding his camera in one hand and gesturing at the people gathered in the church basement with the other. "Let's sit Glinda and the Wizard in the middle and then the rest of you form a half circle behind them."

"Oh, for heaven's sake, Gil," Aunty Em exclaimed. "Enough is enough."

"Darn tootin'," an elderly lady named Martha added. "Elmer here's probably getting a thrill from posing for pictures with us, but Karin's got better things to do with her day than smiling through another roll of film."

"No, really. I'm fine," Karin assured them and smiled at Elmer Brinkley, her co–grand marshal. The circuit-court judge was dressed as the Wizard of Oz. "Though Elmer might have other plans for the morning."

"I can't think of a better way to spend my time than surrounded by the town's most beautiful women," the old man said.

The older women snorted, but Karin kept her smile in place. Just the slightest change in it might send it crashing altogether. She wasn't sure why, but then she wasn't sure of much these days.

She wasn't certain how it happened that she and Jed made love last night. It had been incredible, but she wasn't sure how she felt about it. And she certainly wasn't sure what that strange fluttery feeling in her throat was, except that it wasn't the baby this time.

She was sure, however, that posing for festival PR pictures for the local newspaper was much better than being at home, where her heart would race each time he spoke to her, where her body would flush if she looked at him, and her breath would stop for wanting his touch.

"That's it, folks," the photographer said. "Thanks a lot."

The women sighed and moved away from the pose, Elmer moved along with them. Karin followed the photographer.

"Where to now, Gil?" she asked.

In the last three hours, they'd posed with the town council, the festival committees and even a few of the town's service organizations. The last thing she wanted to do was stop now.

"That's it," the photographer said. "You're free until the Oz show at the grade school this afternoon."

"But that's hours from now," Karin said, glancing at the clock.

The photographer shrugged. "I've got to get pictures

of the construction at the tollway interchange, and of the town's new garbage truck.''

''I could come along,'' she offered.

He gave her a questioning look. ''What for? Glinda in a backhoe? Glinda and the garbage truck?''

Okay, so her coming along didn't make much sense. It was still better than facing Jed when her stomach was square-dancing in big heavy boots at just the thought of his name. If only she knew how he felt about last night, it would help her decide how she felt.

''You and your honey have words?'' Aunty Em asked.

Karin turned, wondering if she was so easy to read or if the older woman was just perceptive. ''No, of course not,'' Karin said with a laugh. ''I want to make sure I'm fulfilling my grand-marshal duties.''

''Uh-huh. I'd almost believe it if Elmer was offering to have his picture taken with a bulldozer, too.''

Karin leaned down closer to the old woman. ''Maybe Elmer doesn't have the same civic pride as I do.''

Aunty Em gave her a look. ''Well, for sure he doesn't have a good-looking cowboy at home to distract him.'' She nodded at Karin's costume. ''If you're looking for ways to waste time, you can change out of that frilly dress and we'll let you help us paint our ornaments.''

''I'm not looking for ways to waste time,'' Karin felt duty-bound to protest. ''But I'd be happy to help you paint.''

''Call it what you want,'' Aunty Em said.

She was calling it like it was, Karin told herself as she changed out of her costume and back into stretch pants and a loose shirt. She wasn't avoiding Jed, she just wasn't seeking him out until she understood her reaction to last night.

She hung up her costume and went back out into the church basement where the informal women's group met. Every year for as long as Karin could remember, they sold Wizard of Oz ornaments at the festival to raise money for holiday baskets for the area's needy. Helping them paint their ornaments was not a way to waste time but to do some good for the community. Karin sat down at an empty place at the table.

"You want to paint the Tinman silver?" Aunty Em asked.

"Sure. I can do that."

Karin picked up a brush and began to dab silver paint on a wooden Tinman. Looks like you didn't have to be made of tin to not have a heart.

She wondered if her lovemaking had been lacking. Of course, it really had not been making love, but still, she wondered if that was why Jed had been moody this morning. Had he been comparing last night to nights he'd spent with his wife and found the memories painful?

Not that she had been trying to compete in any way. Heavens no. But the idea that she had been lacking was oddly bothersome. Especially since the night had been so disquieting for her.

"So how is that young man of yours?" Aunty Em asked. "Has he recovered from his square-dancing incident yet?"

Karin started slightly, jolted from her thoughts. "He's fine," she said. "Still has a slight limp but he claims he always limps a little."

"So what's the trouble?" Mary asked.

"There's no trouble," Karin insisted.

"Maybe he's limping in other ways," Aunty Em said.

"That could get a girl down," someone else agreed.

Karin wasn't sure what they were talking about at first, then she suddenly got their meaning and blushed a bright red. "No, it's not that," she said quickly. The room fell silent and all eyes were on her. She tried to smile. "Really. We're fine. Happy as clams."

The silence lasted a long moment, as did the frowning stares aimed at her. She began to feel a little nervous.

Suddenly Aunty Em nodded. "It's his wife, isn't it? Dang, we should have thought of that."

"You feeling like you're fighting a memory, are you?"

"That's a tough one, all right."

Karin had no idea how they jumped to this topic, but she'd really prefer they jumped to another. "You're all so kind," she said. "But I'm not competing with Wendy."

"Best not to try," Mary agreed. "Just be patient."

"And Lissa loves you. That's important."

"You got time on your side," Aunty Em said.

Karin stopped breathing. She didn't have time on her side at all. It was Thursday and they'd be leaving on Sunday. But then her breath came, along with a jolt of sanity. What was she thinking? Time didn't matter. Last night didn't matter. This was all pretend.

Jed and his memories would go back to Los Angeles and she'd go back to Chicago. Just the way they planned.

Jed followed Marge into the school auditorium. He would have been satisfied to take a seat in the far back, but she wanted to be right up front.

"We have to make sure Lissa knows we're here," Marge pointed out. "I wouldn't want her to think her grandma didn't care."

Jed felt another knife plunge into his heart. Was he hurting too many good people with this charade?

"How about these?" Marge asked. The second row had two empty seats at the end. "I can get good pictures from here."

"Pictures?" Jed sank into his chair.

She pulled a camera from her purse. "I bought it yesterday. I wanted to get a video camera but I had no idea what to get so I settled for this. Do you know much about video cameras? I really should get one before the festival starts tomorrow."

The knives weren't just plunging in anymore, they were plunging and twisting and turning.

"Maybe that wouldn't be such a good idea," he said slowly.

She turned to take a stack of programs from a little boy in a scarecrow costume. "Thanks, sweetie." She helped herself to a program and passed the others to Jed. "Why not?"

Jed extracted a copy and passed the stack to the woman sitting next to him. How could he stop all this hurt, short of betraying Karin's secret? "It's just that—" he took a deep breath and watched a couple of older kids setting up the microphone on the stage "—you have lots of time to look for the best deal before the baby's born."

She gave him a piercing look. "And you don't think Lissa will feel slighted if I don't get it in time to get pictures of her at the festival?"

There was something in her eyes that made him uneasy. "She's just having too good a time here to think about something like that," he said.

"And, of course, there's always lots of time later to get pictures of her," Marge pointed out. There was an odd tone in her voice now, too. "Speaking of which, when are you two getting married? I never could get an answer out of Karin."

"Uh…" Damn. Hadn't they discussed this? He glanced at the stage, wishing the show would suddenly start, but the kids were still fiddling with the mike. "Actually, we aren't sure."

"You should do it this weekend," Marge said. "Wouldn't that be fun?"

"This weekend?" He stared at her, the horror building. "But we don't have the license or anything."

"I bet Elmer could get you through the red tape."

He didn't even bother to ask who Elmer was. "And there's lots of things we haven't decided yet," he went on. "Where to live. What to do about our jobs. Where Lissa should go to school."

"Minor stuff," Marge said with a dismissive wave of her hand. "When you're in love, those things work out."

"Well, yes."

He took another deep breath but it appeared to contain no oxygen at all. Worse yet was the sudden image of him and Karin together. Of the two of them, along with Lissa and the baby, being a family. And how right it felt, even though he knew it couldn't be.

He tried again. "We don't want to rush into things."

Marge sighed. "It's Karin, isn't it? She's being cautious. I had so hoped she would have the courage to follow her heart."

Jed didn't know what to say, but for once in this whole doomed vacation, luck was with him and the show started. He hadn't known what to expect, but it turned out to be all sorts of skits about L. Frank Baum, what was happening in the country when he wrote *The Wizard of Oz,* and what life in Kansas was like then.

It would have been fairly interesting, except that Karin and some older man were guests of honor and Jed was having trouble keeping his eyes on the kids. Jed had known Karin was going to be Glinda the Good Witch, but he hadn't seen her in her costume yet. And hadn't expected her to look so magically beautiful.

She was wearing a frilly dress in a shade of pink that made her skin glow and her hair seem even darker. She did seem nervous, though, as if she didn't like being the center of attention, and he wished he could tell her to relax. That she was part of the magic of the festival and not to worry.

"She's always been so afraid of emotions," Marge whispered, leaning close to him so she wouldn't disturb the first-graders reciting a poem about Munchkinland.

"Lots of people are," Jed pointed out.

"Not to the extent she is."

The first-graders finished their poem and the audience clapped as parents scrambled to take pictures of the little ones dressed like Munchkins. Then the children trooped off the stage, one little girl lingering near Karin to stare at her in awe.

"She used to believe in magic, too," Marge said softly. "When she was little, she thought the whole world was magic."

Jed kept silent as an older group of students came onstage. They were presenting information about life in Kansas around the turn of the century. Hard, bleak and at the mercy of the elements. But wasn't much of life like that? You had to find happiness where you could.

His eyes strayed to Karin. She wasn't part of his happiness and he wasn't part of hers, but he sure hoped she found some soon. She deserved it. Maybe when the baby came, she would see that she could love. Then maybe she would let herself be loved in return. As for him, his chance at happiness had passed and he wasn't about to try again.

"It was my fault," Marge leaned close again to whisper as the older kids left the stage. "It was all those jerks I married."

Jed looked at her. "What?"

"Karin wanted a father who would be a father to her," Marge said. "So every time I married, she dreamed that this one would be the one to read her stories at bedtime, and check for monsters under her bed. He would teach her to ride her bike and tell her she was beautiful."

Jed nodded as the next class came on. "But they didn't?"

"They didn't know how to be husbands, let alone fathers," she said, bitterness coming through in her voice. "Neither of us got what we needed, but she was the one more hurt in the long run. Once I saw that, I stopped falling for every twinkling pair of blue eyes."

He looked up at Karin, greeting a new class on the stage. "But she never bounced back, did she?"

"The monsters are still under her bed, though she pretends they aren't."

"We all have monsters we're fighting."

"But they are easier to fight when you've got someone with you.'' Marge grabbed his hand and held it tightly. ''Don't let her push you away, Jed. She loves you and you love her. I can tell. Fight for that love.''

He couldn't have spoken to save his life. He wanted to tell her that she was wrong on all counts, but his heart knew better.

Dorothy hadn't ever really realized how special the festival was until she had moved away. Now each little moment was one to treasure. She saw Heather leading her kindergarten class from the auditorium and waved to her.

Heather paused. ''Wasn't that fun? Karin did a great job.''

''She was perfect,'' Dorothy agreed. ''And the costume you made her looked wonderful.''

Heather nodded away the praise. ''She made it come alive.''

With a slight wave, Heather led her class toward her classroom and Dorothy went around to the locker room where Karin was changing out of her costume. Karin had been wonderful with the kids, so animated, so into the role. Loving Jed and Lissa had changed Karin. Made her softer, more gentle.

Maybe it was just that Dorothy was feeling so glum herself. Only three more days and she was leaving again.

Karin came out of the locker room, her costume over her arm. ''Hey,'' she said, stopping when she saw Dorothy. ''I didn't know you were here.''

Dorothy forced her moodiness away. ''Are you kidding? This is the unofficial beginning of the festival. I couldn't miss it.''

Karin made a face. "Come on, this is pretty tame compared to what you can see in Paris."

"That doesn't make it less enjoyable. In fact, I liked it better than a lot of stuff I've seen in Paris."

Karin shook her head. "You must be feverish," she said. They started walking toward the exit.

"It's not that easy to settle in a new place," Dorothy said. "You probably found that out when you moved to Chicago."

Karin gave her a look that seemed to go right through her. "You're not happy there."

"Of course I am," Dorothy protested and pushed open the outside door.

The parking lot was practically deserted. There was no one around to overhear them talking so this would be the time to confess all to Karin—if there was something to confess, of course.

"Paris is great," Dorothy went on. "It's exciting. I am the envy of the whole town, or so Toto tells me. How could I not be happy?"

"Maybe because you'd rather Toto tell you how much he misses you."

Dorothy's laughter died, turning into an annoyed glare, though the annoyance was more for herself. Was she that transparent?

"Just because you're head over heels in love, it doesn't mean the rest of us are, too," she told Karin.

Karin seemed to pale slightly as she stopped walking. "I'm not head over heels in love," she said, her voice faltering.

Dorothy stopped too. "Oh, come on, both you and Jed light up when the other comes near. You don't notice anyone else is around. And you have this glow about you."

Karin didn't appear to see the humor in it. "It's makeup."

Dorothy wasn't going to back down. Karin had always been so defensive about her feelings. "I couldn't decide which was cuter in the show today," Dorothy said. "The way you kept watching Jed, or the way he kept watching you."

Panic seemed to flit through Karin's eyes, but she just smiled. "I think the cutest thing is the way you and Toto avoid looking at each other at all. And then when your eyes do meet, you both go bright red."

Dorothy felt as if the air had been knocked from her. "We do not."

Karin's smile changed, softened. Her eyes turned sad as she put a hand on Dorothy's. "What would you say if I told you Toto's been seeing someone else?"

Dorothy's heart stopped. Totally. It just cracked in two and broke. She stared at Karin for the longest time. Why hadn't anyone told her? She wouldn't have come back. No, she had to come for Penny and Brad's wedding, but then she would have left right away. She would never have stayed to be an object of pity around town.

She made herself smile somehow. "That's wonderful," she said. "Is it anyone I know? I'm so happy for him."

Karin frowned. "He isn't and you're not," she said. "But if you keep dragging your feet, one of these days he will be seeing someone else."

It had been a trick? Dorothy tried to be angry, tried to be insulted. Tried to be anything but hurt and scared. She couldn't seem to muster anything strong enough to fight the fear.

"I'm not the one dragging my feet," she said.

"Oh, no?" Karin shifted her costume onto the other arm. "You're waiting for your prince to show up and turning Toto away because he doesn't have a fancy enough carriage or enough horses."

Dorothy stared at her friend. "Where in the world did you come up with that?" she asked. "People in love always think everyone else is in love too, but it's just not true."

"This has nothing to do with me," Karin said. "Your and Toto's feelings for each other are obvious."

"Not to those of us without the rose-colored glasses," Dorothy said.

Karin frowned at her, biting her lip as if trying to make a decision. Finally, she put her hand on Dorothy's arm. "Walk with me to my car, will you?"

Dorothy glanced around them. There was no one else in sight, so why the need for secrecy? But she walked along at Karin's side.

"You might be right about people in love assuming others are too," Karin said slowly. "But you're wrong to lump me with them."

Dorothy stared at her. "Huh? You're trying to tell me you aren't in love with Jed?"

"I'm not," Karin said. They'd reached the car and, after putting the costume in the back, she turned to Dorothy once more. "And he's not in love with me. Our engagement isn't for real."

Dorothy blinked once, as if this was a dream and that would take her back to reality. Nothing changed though. Karin was still staring at her, uncertainty in her eyes.

"I think I missed something here," Dorothy said slowly. "What in the world are you talking about?"

Karin glanced around nervously as if she was afraid

of being overheard. Or else she was just having trouble meeting Dorothy's eyes.

"Someone got the wrong idea at the hospital after we were caught in the storm and Jed came with me to the wedding to set it straight. Except then, my mother and everybody were so excited there didn't seem to be a way to tell the truth."

"So you've been pretending to be engaged all week?" This was unbelievable. Dorothy glanced down and frowned. "What about the baby? Is that make-believe too?"

Karin shook her head. "But it's not Jed's. I first met him last Saturday."

Dorothy leaned against the car, her legs not certain they could hold her up. "Let me get this straight. You met this guy on Saturday and convinced him to pretend to be engaged to you?" She started to laugh. "This is wild."

"It is not," Karin whispered sharply. "It was just an…an arrangement."

"An arrangement?" Dorothy repeated, still laughing. "And are you going to pretend to get married, too?"

"Of course not," Karin snapped. "Once the festival is over, he goes back to Los Angeles and I'll tell Mom that we broke up."

Dorothy stopped laughing and stood away from the car. "Why? Isn't his carriage big enough or doesn't he have enough horses?"

"What are you—" Karin stopped with a definite frown. "It's not the same thing at all. Mine has been all pretense. Totally. Every minute of the past week. I'm the Tinman, remember? I don't have a heart to lose."

Dorothy smiled at her. "So every minute was fake?" she asked. Her smile deepened at the shadow that crossed Karin's face. "There wasn't one moment when you forgot you were pretending?"

Karin began to dig in her purse. "Of course not. I knew what I was getting into." She pulled out her car keys. "I really need to get going. Mom's hosting the school's corn-roast dinner at the bar tonight and I need to help her."

"Sure." Dorothy stepped away from the car. "I'll see you there."

Jed came into the bar's kitchen just as Karin was leaving it, a tray of clean silverware in her hands. He took it from her and leaned close.

"We really need to talk, darlin'," he said, his voice ripe with urgency.

It was the urgency that made her spine tingle, Karin told herself. Nothing else. Certainly not his use of the word *darlin'*. She had spent the day getting herself in control and she wasn't losing it now.

"In a minute," she said and took the tray back from him. "I'll take these out front. You bring more sweet corn outside."

She hurried past him through the bar and out to the tables of food set up on the sidewalk in front. The cornstalks had been pulled away from the buildings and scattered about the sidewalk and blocked-off street. It was ready to be part of the traveling *Wizard of Oz* production tomorrow, but tonight tables had been added to accommodate the annual corn roast for the elementary-school library.

And it was a big job. Her mother had lots of volunteer help, but there still was plenty for Karin to do.

So it wasn't that she was avoiding Jed, but she wasn't actually seeking him out, either. She was just so mixed up. Last night was wonderful, no doubt about it. But then this morning was awkward and just when she thought she was getting things worked out in her head, she spilled the beans to Dorothy. Of course, Dorothy was all wrong about everything—neither of them was in love.

Karin dumped the silverware tray on the buffet table and began to refill the individual bins.

"This is going to be some busy weekend," someone said to her.

"If you need anything, just ask," someone else said.

Karin smiled and nodded. This wasn't the first time this evening someone had offered their help. Why would this weekend be any busier than any other festival weekend? They must have thought she had more to do because she was a grand marshal. Elmer Brinkley was coming out of the bar when Karin was going back in.

"Ah, the lady of the hour," he said as he stepped aside. "That special license will be no problem, either. Just tell me when you need it."

With a pat on her arm, he went on by, leaving her staring after him.

Special license? What special license? She had her driver's license and her medical one. Neither of which needed updating or modifying.

Nancy Abbott stopped and gave her a mighty hug. "This is so great," she said. "Just say the word and I'll organize the flowers."

"What word?" Karin asked.

But Nancy just laughed and went over to get her food. Karin was too confused to move for a moment, then turned as she felt a hand on her arm. It was Jed. For a split second, her confusion fled as she was awash in fever, longing, embarrassment and awareness.

"What is going on?" she asked in a harsh whisper. "People are making the strangest comments to me."

He put the silverware tray on an empty table, then took Karin's hand and led her away from the buffet.

"There go the lovebirds," someone called out.

"Just remember that's not a real field," someone else said.

"And that there are kids around."

Jed just laughed and smiled, but Karin was too conscious of her hand in his, and the fact that there was no real reason for the teasing. She told herself she was glad, but that didn't explain the dread lurking behind her stiff smile.

Once they were in the relative seclusion of the make-believe cornfield, surrounded by tall, dried cornstalks, Jed let go of her hand. She stuck both her hands in the pocket of her apron.

"So what's this all about?" she asked.

"Well, darlin', it's like this. Your mother wants us to get married this weekend."

Chapter Ten

"She what?" Karin cried, trying to keep her voice low. She tried to say something—anything—else, but her mouth didn't seem to work. The idea was appalling, terrifying, tantalizing. And utterly impossible.

"I guess this Elmer guy is some kind of judge," Jed was going on in a quiet voice. "Your mom talked to him about getting a special license, found out the church is available Sunday afternoon and figures she could host a reception in the bar afterward."

"We can't," Karin said, her brain finally allowing a word to come out.

He gave her a look that wondered why she was stating the obvious. Something she wondered herself.

"We'll just tell them it's too fast," she went on, more briskly. "We couldn't get your family here."

"Lissa's the only family I have left," he said. "We'll say you want your co-workers to be there."

She shook her head. "No one will believe that. I haven't taken the time to make many friends through work. Not personal ones that I'd want at my wedding."

There was a burst of laughter nearby. Too close for comfort, though Karin doubted anyone was listening to them. Jed took her arm and pulled her farther into the cornfield.

"So what do we do?" he whispered.

She bit her lip, trying to think. It was easier once she took a step back from Jed, forcing him to let go of her.

"We could have a fight," she suggested, brushing a corn leaf away from the back of her neck.

He nodded slowly, as if giving the idea some thought. "That might work. What would we fight about?"

"About where we'll live after we're married," Karin said. How had that come to her so fast? It wasn't as if she had given the matter any thought. Or not much, anyway.

"You want to move out to L.A.," Jed said. "And I don't want you to give up your practice."

She stared at him with a frown. It was starting to get dark and his face was in the shadows. He was joking, he had to be. Would he really give up his life in L.A.—

Wait, what was she thinking? This was all pretend.

She crossed her arms over her chest, as if that would keep her head together. "Or how about you want to buy a horse farm out here but don't want me to help pay for it?"

"I wouldn't," he agreed. His voice sounded almost belligerent.

"Why not?" she asked. "It would be my home, too."

"A husband provides a home for his wife."

She found his words disturbing and swatted impatiently at a pesky fly. "So he has to pay for it?"

"That's what providing is."

"Even if I make more money than you?"

"I don't do badly."

She couldn't believe that he felt this way. It was so...so...old-fashioned and dumb. "But you don't have enough cash for a ranch."

"So it would take a few more years, what's the big rush?"

"There's no rush, but it's stupid to wait when I have the money now."

"It's stupid to want to take care of your own?" he snapped. "Or do you just like the power that comes along with a big income?"

"You're blowing this all out of proportion. Once we're married—"

She stopped, her words echoing in the air around them as the world turned totally still. The crowd on the other side of the cornfield seemed to have disappeared. Or were they all listening in?

For a moment she couldn't breathe, but then she made herself laugh. "Well, I guess we could do an argument pretty convincingly."

He nodded, looking as if he needed a deep breath too. "Yeah." His voice was low. "That went pretty well. Maybe we were even overheard."

"Wouldn't that be a break?" She wasn't sure she wanted to re-create that, assuming she even could. "Actually, I'd be surprised if we—"

She stopped, her hand going down to her stomach.

The baby was doing aerobics all of a sudden. It felt so strange, but wonderfully so. She grabbed Jed's hand and put it on her stomach where the baby was kicking.

"Feel this," she said with a laugh. "What do you think? Soccer player or football punter?"

He smiled, a warm secret smile that touched her in places she couldn't name. He was still a moment, feeling the movement beneath his hand. "Could be a ballerina, darlin'. Or maybe a figure skater."

"Better than a rock climber."

"Or a rock star."

"A rock star?" She had sudden visions of her child dressed in leather hounded by groupies and singing songs with lyrics she couldn't understand. "Isn't there a vaccination or something for that?"

He laughed and suddenly she was in his arms. It was the most magical place to be. A place where dreams were possible and the wildest wishes would come true. His lips came down on hers and she felt as if she was on a Ferris wheel, riding high up into the stars. A dizzy and dancing feeling was in the air, and she felt as if she could touch the sky.

Then his kiss changed, deepened, grew harder, as if he was needing something only she could give. It sent a shiver all through her, but it also awoke a deepening hunger, a call to rest in his arms and be totally one with him. Memories of last night echoed around her and she felt herself being swept away by them.

But he pulled away slowly, regretfully. "I'm sorry, darlin'," he said.

She nodded, not quite up to words yet. A deep breath helped, and so did staring at the cornstalk next to Jed instead of at him. Her knees felt weak and she wasn't sure she had a voice, but away from the spell he cast over her, she felt more herself.

"It's okay," she said. "Let's just hope we weren't seen. It wouldn't have added anything to our argument."

"We need to be more careful," he said. "I need to be."

"No, we both do." She wasn't letting him take the blame.

He sighed and stuck his hands in the pockets of his jeans. "About last night." He cleared his throat. "That shouldn't have happened either."

"No." He was right but somehow it hurt to have him say so.

"Not that it wasn't wonderful," he added quickly.

His words eased the hurt a bit. "It was," she agreed. "But it was just hormones on my part."

"And I guess I was lonelier than I realized." He gave her a smile that sent little tremors through her. "But now that we know what caused it, we can make sure it doesn't happen again."

"Right. We can be more careful."

"And it'll be even easier since we've had our argument."

"I almost forgot about that." She pulled all the fraying pieces of her sanity back together. "You're a stubborn chauvinistic jerk."

"And you're flaunting your success."

She nodded, feeling strangely alone all of a sudden. The irritation wasn't there anymore and the words just seemed to build a wall between them. "Well, it's been fun," she said.

"Yeah, it has, darlin'."

He sounded almost surprised, but she was not going

to dwell on that. Just as she was not going to dwell on the sense of loss making her want to cry. She turned and walked out of the cornfield.

Her mother met her at the door to the bar. "There you are, sweetie," Marge said. "Did Jed tell you about my little idea?"

Karin took a deep breath. "That chauvinistic jerk?" she said. "I don't want to talk about it."

"Karin!" her mother cried, but Karin just kept on walking. Why did she feel she was betraying part of herself?

"Jed? What are you doing out here?" Marge asked.

Jed sat up on the sofa, barely able to open his eyes. Damn, he was getting tired of these games. He couldn't sleep when he was in the bedroom and so close to Karin, but once he exiled himself to the sofa in the living room, he couldn't because she was too far away. Thank goodness the festival started today and this whole thing was almost over.

He forced himself to smile at Marge. "Morning, ma'am," he said brightly. "I trust you slept well. It was a fine cookout in the cornfield."

"Don't try to change the subject. You two can't still be arguing."

"I'm afraid this is serious, ma'am," he said, feeling a bit like a scoundrel. He picked up his jeans and pulled them on over his boxers. "It's a real sticking point for both of us."

"Oh, fiddlesticks," she snapped. "It's Karin dragging her feet, isn't it? You can't let her do it."

"There are some things a man's got to stand up for." Half-dressed, he picked up his sheet and pillow.

"If thing's aren't going to work out, best to know it now."

"But there's a baby involved," she cried.

Jed clutched the bedclothes closer to his chest. "A man's got to respect himself before he can expect it from anyone else." Why did the words seem to be so hard to hear, coming from his own lips?

"I thought better of you," she muttered. "I thought you were different than those jerks I married." She gave him a withering look, then stomped off into the bathroom, slamming the door.

Jed sighed and dropped the bedclothes back onto the sofa. He went into the kitchen to start the coffee. Not that it was going to help him feel less like something that ought to be run out of town, but maybe he'd feel more awake for his hanging.

"Daddy," Lissa said.

He turned. She was standing in the kitchen doorway, holding Marge's cat and frowning at him.

"Why, good morning, darlin'." The one bright spot in his life. He went over and kissed the top of her head but she stayed stiff.

"Are you and Karin still fighting?" she asked.

He pulled away from her, glancing over toward the bathroom. The shower was still running, so it was safe to talk. Stooping down so he was eye level with Lissa, he smiled at her.

"It's just part of our little game," he said. "You know, make-believe."

"So you aren't mad at each other?" Lissa persisted.

He shook his head. "Nope."

Lissa visibly relaxed, her normal smile breaking out on her lips. "That's good," she said. "I was worried."

That worried him. "Why?" he asked. "You know this is just pretend."

"Yeah, but I like Karin. She treats me like I'm not just a little kid." She put the cat down on a kitchen chair and then went over to the cabinet to get a box of cereal. Not Crunchy Flakes, but a competitor's. She poured herself a bowl, then got the milk out of the refrigerator. "I think she'd be a great mother, don't you?"

"Sure," Jed said carefully, not certain where this was going. "But this is just a little game for while we are in town."

Lissa brought her bowl over to the table and sat down next to the cat. "I like Chesterton," she said and spooned a little bit of cereal onto the table in front of the cat. "Here you go, Shilah," she said softly then, once the cat started to eat, looked back at Jed. "Everybody's really nice here."

His worries were growing. He took the seat across the table from her. "Lissa, we have a life back in Los Angeles. You have friends there, and a school you like, and your job for Crunchy Flakes."

"But it hasn't felt like home since Mommy died," she said and swallowed a spoonful of cereal herself. "And Crunchy Flakes isn't forever. Aaron says they think I'm starting to look too old and they want me to wear dumb little-kid clothes. I don't know if I want to sign another contract with them."

Jed wasn't surprised though her agent hadn't mentioned that to him. "How long you stay with Crunchy Flakes has always been your decision," he said. "But that doesn't change the fact that our life is in California."

She stopped eating, a flicker of hope in her eyes. "If

we moved here, you could go back to riding in the rodeo and I could stay with Grandma.''

He stared at her, his stomach being eaten away by dread. ''Lissa, honey,'' he said softly. ''You know she's not your grandmother. You know this is all pretend.''

''But it doesn't have to be. You said you like Karin.''

''Yes, but that doesn't mean we should change our lives around.''

''Changing them could make them better,'' she pointed out and gave the cat another spoonful of cereal.

''Only if you change them because of love,'' he said. ''And I'm not in love with Karin.''

''How do you know?''

Because he was never loving again. But he couldn't explain that to Lissa. ''Because when you love somebody, you stop being who you are and become somebody else.''

She stopped eating to give him a confused look. ''You mean you wouldn't be a cowboy anymore?''

It wasn't exactly what he meant, but how did you explain to an eight-year-old that love makes you better, stronger, more complete until you weren't the same anymore? ''And since I'm still me,'' he said, ''we're still leaving here the day after tomorrow like we planned.''

Her eyes turned stormy and her jaw took on that stubborn tension he knew only too well. ''But I don't want to go,'' she cried. ''That is so not fair. How come I don't get a vote?''

How had things gotten out of hand like this? ''Because it's not a topic for discussion,'' he snapped.

She jumped up, grabbed Shilah in her arms and gave

him a look hot enough to melt sand. ''You are a mean, mean daddy and I'm never ever going to like you again.'' She turned and ran from the room.

Jed sighed and braced himself for the inevitable slamming of the bedroom door. He still flinched when it happened, but he went on cleaning up the remains of Lissa's breakfast. She was mad at him, but she'd get over it. Once they got back home, she'd forget all about this place. Just as he would.

''Lots of door slamming going on here.''

He turned. Karin was in the doorway. Dressed in a cotton robe and slippers, she still looked so beautiful it took his breath away. Lucky he'd been careful. It would have been all too easy to fall in love with her.

''Good morning,'' he said. ''Are you sure you want to associate with me? I'm on just about everybody's bad side.''

''Poor baby.'' She laughed and poured herself a glass of orange juice. ''What have you been doing to get everyone so ticked off at you?''

''Just being myself,'' he admitted and sat down. He wasn't so sure he wanted to elaborate. ''So the festival starts today. I can't wait.''

She came over and sat down, giving him a look that clearly said he was nuts, but he didn't care. He had to get his mind off her.

''So what are you doing this morning?'' he asked, trying hard not to notice how cozy this all was. Or how right it felt. He liked starting the day with someone, that was all. ''I know there's an opening ceremony this afternoon and a dinner tonight, but I thought if you weren't booked up already, we could do something this morning.''

"Wouldn't that kind of spoil the effect of our argument?"

Damn, that was dumb. How could he have forgotten? "Yeah, you're right," he said quickly. "And we don't want to stage that over again. It was hard enough to be convincing the first time."

"I didn't think it was that hard," she said. "All you have to do is get all macho again and we'll be fighting."

"Just what does 'getting macho' mean?" he asked.

She put down her orange juice and frowned at him. "Oh, come on. You know what it is. Getting all bossy and caveman-like. The big man in charge of the little woman."

That stung. "I was not being the big man in charge of the little woman," he said irately. "And I don't see how wanting to take care of my family is being bossy or caveman-like."

"It is when you get all huffy about using a woman's earnings."

"Given your mother's experiences, I would think you'd appreciate a man who wants to pay your way. Or are you only attracted to men that you can have under your thumb?"

She paled at his words. And so did he. What had possessed him—

"That's a terrible thing to say," she cried and got to her feet.

"It was," he agreed quickly and got to his feet also. He couldn't tell if she was angry or on the verge of tears, but prayed it was anger. He couldn't take tears. "I'm sorry. I don't know why I said it."

"Maybe it's just as well we've argued," she said. "It certainly is going to make the next few days easier to get through. No more need to pretend we care about each other.''

Suddenly her anger wasn't that much easier to bear. ''I really am sorry,'' he said again. ''It was just the stress talking.''

''The stress?'' she snapped. ''Of what? Pretending to care about me? Oh, that certainly is nice to hear.''

Jeez, she wouldn't give him a break. ''Well, it hasn't been a picnic. Not the kind of vacation a travel agent would book for me.''

''Nobody forced you to stay.''

''Just my sense of honor.''

''Oh, spare me,'' she cried and, turning on her heel, marched from the room. Another door slammed.

He sank back into his chair. A few hours' walking around town and he should have everyone in Chesterton mad at him.

At least he was free of the pretend engagement. He should be relieved. So why wasn't he?

''I now declare the Oz festival has begun,'' Karin said loudly and cut the ribbon.

The covering came off a large cake constructed to look like Dorothy's house after it landed in Oz, and everyone cheered. Karin pretended to also, but hoped no one was watching her too closely. She wasn't in the mood for all this partying.

They were in the library parking lot, where Munch-kinland had been set up. At the start of the yellow brick–painted road, a small stage had been placed for the opening ceremony. Karin and Elmer, in their costumes, were on it along with Betsy McKinley, the festival chair this year. The townsfolk, most of them in Oz costumes, were gathered around the stage.

"Mrs. Brewster is going to cut the cake now," Betsy announced to the crowd. "So get in line for your piece."

Karin and Elmer, as grand marshals of the festival, got their slices first and Karin tried to eat hers, but her mood for cake was about as nonexistent as her mood for partying. She tried to look happy and excited and enthusiastic about her role as Glinda the Good Witch, but all she could think about was that she hadn't been very nice to Jed that morning.

He'd been right about that whole money issue. She should be pleased to learn there were men out there who didn't want some woman to pay their way. From her mother's experiences, she wouldn't think there were. She would think that all men were out to use women and then move on. But Jed wasn't like that and rather than commend him for being different, she had given him hell for it.

"Is something wrong with the cake?" Mrs. Brewster asked.

Karin started and realized that the woman had been staring at her, and her untouched piece of cake. "No, it's fine," Karin assured her and took a bite. "It's great."

The ceremony was over. Just the mingling and posing for pictures were left for the moment. She put down her cake on the railing around the back of the stage and went on into the crowd.

"How wonderful you look," someone said to her.

"Like a princess, not a witch," someone else said.

"Where's your young man?" a woman asked.

"You aren't still quarreling, are you?"

Karin went through the crowd, smiling and nodding and listening to advice from everyone. Don't let a man get the best of you. Nothing's worth risking your love for. Learn to compromise. Make him an apple pie.

If only it was that simple, she thought with a sigh. Not that any of these ideas really were apropos since she and Jed weren't in love. But still, she didn't like having anger lying between them.

"Hi, Karin. Gosh, you look so cool."

Karin turned to find Lissa and her friends beside her. Lissa was dressed as Dorothy, while two of her friends were scarecrows and another was the Cowardly Lion. Karin was going to miss the girl. It had been fun to share girl talk over meals. But she wasn't going to think of things that couldn't be.

"You guys look pretty great yourselves." Karin took a deep breath for courage. "Is your dad here?"

Lissa's face darkened slightly. "No, I came with Ginger. Daddy said he was going to watch the bar for Grandma."

"That was nice of him." That was such a big part of the problem—he was just a really nice guy.

"I guess," Lissa said, apparently not ready to forgive him herself. "Grandma said he could because she wanted to come take pictures, but she said she was still mad at him."

The poor guy. He couldn't win, and it had all started so innocently. Maybe it was time to unbend a little. There wasn't any love to protect, but she could bring him some cake.

She hurried back up onto the stage, slipped in behind the cake table and took a fresh piece of cake and the slice that had been cut for her earlier. She couldn't keep a smile from her lips and a bounce from her step as she hurried through the crowd, and over the few blocks to her mother's bar.

* * *

Jed turned off the television in the corner and sank onto a bar stool to finish reading the newspaper. It wasn't the local paper that had been delivered that morning—that was filled with festival news and pictures of Karin. Or was it just mentions of her? Or maybe it hadn't even been that. Maybe they had implied her presence, but it was too much either way.

So he'd walked to the drugstore and bought a copy of the *Chicago Tribune*. Fine paper. Good paper. Not one mention of the *Wizard of Oz* in it. So why was he finding it boring as hell?

Almost as boring as manning the bar this afternoon. Marge had said she would just close, but he hadn't wanted to see her lose business so he'd offered to run it for her. Big favor. How was he supposed to know everyone in this town attended every festival function? Oh well, at least his absence was helping the town to accept his and Karin's breakup. That was a bonus, even if it didn't exactly feel like one.

He wandered over to the wall where Marge's cowboy-hat collection was hanging. He plucked one off a hook and looked at it. It was a nice one but not new. Where did Marge get them? Did she steal them off sleeping cowboys' heads? He'd have to keep a close eye on his own.

The bell on the door rang as it was opened and he spun around. It was Karin. His heart leaped as he tossed the hat back on its hook.

"Boy, you look busy," she said. Her tone was light and laughing.

He smiled in return. "You wouldn't believe the crowds."

"That amazing, huh?" She closed the door after her and seemed to glide across the room. Maybe that was how witches walked. "I brought you some cake. It's a corner of Dorothy's house."

"Thanks." He took it from her. Cake had never looked so good before. "Sorry I missed the ceremony. How did it go?"

"I was splendid." She sat down at a table and grinned at him, sending his heart into overdrive. "A cake was never unveiled so expertly."

"Surgical precision, I take it?"

"The *Journal of the American Medical Association* sent a reporter. Aren't you going to have your cake?"

"Oh. Yeah. Right." He sat down and picked up the plastic fork she'd brought. "You sure this won't wreck the story we've been building?"

"Everyone's at the ceremony still," she said and started eating her own piece. "No one was paying any attention to me."

She had a little smear of icing on her upper lip that seemed to hypnotize him. He had the strongest urge to wipe it off with his finger. To kiss it off. To—

He took a deep breath and concentrated on his cake. "Great cake," he said brightly. "Never knew a house could taste so good."

"I'm glad you like it. House has always been my favorite flavor."

"Mine too, but you can't get it much back in L.A. More skyscraper cakes than house ones."

"What a bummer."

"That's for sure." He ate the rest of the cake with lightness riding high in his heart. How was it she was so easy to talk to?

"I'm sorry about this morning," she said, catching him off guard as she pushed her plate away. "I shouldn't have taken insult."

"I shouldn't have said what I did."

"Why not? You were right. I don't know about Mom's thinking, but I'm sure keeping power would be important to me in a relationship. I saw too often what happens when you give it up."

He pushed his plate away and leaned back in his chair. "No," he said softly. "You saw what happened when you didn't. Your mom never gave up power, and she lost always. She didn't trust."

"Didn't trust?" Karin's laugh was tinged with bitterness. "She trusted too easily, I'd say."

He shook his head. "If she went into a relationship believing the guy had to carry part of it, she never would have stayed with any of them. She felt if she carried the whole load, they would love her more and that's not how love works."

"No, I guess not." She rubbed her stomach absently. "Maybe she knows as little about love as I do."

"But you'll learn." He scooted his chair closer to hers. "Junior practicing acrobatics again?"

She nodded, putting his hand on her stomach. He could feel the baby moving, but his eyes were on her face. The wonder and awe there were spellbinding. He was only vaguely aware of the baby, his heart was filled with her.

"You're going to be all right," he said. "You know that, don't you?"

She shrugged but the soft smile stayed on her lips. "I'm starting to think I might be," she admitted. "But still a little scared."

"It's okay to be."

She nodded. "I've got a lot of thinking and planning to do. But Mom'll be here to help. All I have to do is ask."

"She'll be a wonderful grandmother. Just ask Lissa."

Karin's smile faltered slightly. A little of the sun slipped from the room. "Lissa's mad at you, you know."

"Part of being a parent. You'll find that out soon enough."

"It's probably my fault."

"That she's mad at me?" He wasn't going to go into her reasons. "No, she's mad because I'm a mean, mean dad. We'll survive, don't worry."

He leaned over and touched her lips with his. It was a gentle kiss, a tender kiss, a kiss that could go on forever. His heart soared into flight, but he brought it back down to earth and pulled away.

"Thanks for everything," she said softly. Her eyes were glowing as if life was filled with sunshine.

"Sure." His felt filled with rain.

Chapter Eleven

Karin braced herself as the convertible slowly went around the corner. It probably wouldn't do for one of the festival grand marshals to tumble off the back of her car in the parade. Her smile grew a little wider as she continued to wave to the crowds along the parade route.

Little kids, teens, adults and elders, most dressed in Oz costumes, were lining the streets. They were all waving to her and Elmer, and taking pictures. Behind their car was the Chesterton High School marching band, and then came floats and civic groups and social clubs and sports teams, some antique cars and tractors and more.

"Good crowd this year," Elmer said to her.

"Seems like it."

Actually, Karin hadn't been back for the festival for several years and she had never been in a position to judge the size of the crowds. Even so, the interest she had today in the crowds wasn't so much in their size as in whom she was passing. So far, she hadn't seen Jed or Lissa and the parade was almost over.

But then, over near the park, she saw them. Jed standing so tall and Lissa looking so excited. The little girl was beside herself waving and shouting to Karin, while Jed just smiled at her. And the smile seemed to melt her heart into—

She stopped, frozen in half wave. Her heart? She put her hand on the frilly pink sash around her waist, but it wasn't the baby she was feeling. It was something else.

She looked back over at Jed and felt that stirring again, that sense of wonder and expansion and amazement. She felt infinitely rich and more alive than she ever had before.

Not only did she have a heart, she was in love. And it was wonderful. Maybe she ought to be shocked or scared or in denial, but she couldn't be. It truly felt wonderful. She wanted to dance and sing and shout it out to everyone.

But all she did was give Jed a slight wave and smile before the car turned another corner and they were lost from sight. Then she spent the time waving to the hundreds of Dorothys along the way as her mind explored this idea of love. To try it on and see if it fit. Or rather, try it on and delight in its newness.

"Nice young man, you've got there," Elmer said to her. "It's obvious that he cares a lot for you."

"Is it?"

Her newly liberated heart did a little dance of joy, twirling in the sunshine of her love. Maybe once this was all over, she and Jed could see each other again.

Maybe they could try to build a real relationship. One based on feelings, not a lie.

Maybe he would like to come to see the baby when it was born. Or even be there when it was, but maybe her dreams were going too wild. Maybe she needed to take it slow and not build up expectations until she had a little more basis for them.

The convertible turned into the junior-high-school parking lot, pulling around into an empty spot to make room for the vehicles behind them. Betsy McKinley hurried over, checking her clipboard.

"Okay, you have two hours," she said. "Then you need to be at the library for the start of the play. Oh, and Karin, there's a reporter who was asking to interview you."

"Sure, why not?"

All Karin had wanted to do was hurry over to see Jed, not to tell him about her feelings just yet, but to be with him. She had other responsibilities though. And maybe he'd be walking over this way to meet her. She could always hope.

Betsy waved a woman over. A photographer trailed behind. "Dr. Spencer says she has time for a few questions," she called out.

Karin had a moment's misgivings as she watched the woman and the photographer come over. She had no idea why her stomach was jittery. The woman was probably in her mid-thirties and dressed well enough, but her eyes glittered with a look that struck Karin as being hungry.

"This is Mary Catherine Cooper," Betsy was saying. "With *Worldwide News*."

The supermarket tabloid? Why would one of those newspapers that traded on the sensational be doing a story on the Wizard of Oz Festival? Karin's feeling of uneasiness grew. She hoped they weren't going to try to sensationalize something about the festival.

"What can I do for you, Ms. Cooper?" Karin asked as the photographer, after a nod from the reporter, started taking pictures. Karin knew her voice sounded cool, but she couldn't shake her worries. "Can we walk as we're talking? I need to get to the next event."

It wasn't strictly true as she had plenty of time to walk the six blocks, but it gave her more control over the interview.

"Whatever works for you, Doctor," the woman said. "And you can call me Cooper. That's what everybody does."

"Fine." Though Karin didn't expect to be talking to her long enough to call her one thing or another.

She lifted her skirts slightly to avoid the gravelly surface of the parking lot and started walking. The reporter walked alongside her, taking out a small tape recorder and flicking it on while the photographer walked backward ahead of them, taking shots as they walked. How many shots did they want, for goodness' sakes?

"Is it true that you're engaged to Jed McCarron?" the woman asked.

It wasn't the type of question Karin expected to be asked. And not one she particularly wanted to answer. Her steps faltered. "I beg your pardon?" she said. "Why in the world would your readers care about that?"

"Just how did you meet Jed and his daughter?" Cooper went on as if Karin hadn't spoken. "Are either of them patients of yours?"

"What in the world are you talking about?" Karin

exclaimed. "I thought this was an interview about the festival."

"You're not denying that you know Jed McCarron and his daughter, Melissa, are you?"

"No, I'm not denying it," Karin snapped. "But I do fail to see what interest it would be to anyone at all."

The woman hurried her steps and turned so she was facing Karin, the tape recorder held out to catch every word. Every nuance.

"The Crunchy Flakes kid is one of the most popular figures in the country," Cooper said. "Our readers want to know all about her."

"All about who?" This interview was turning bizarre. Was it too late to change her mind? "Look, I don't have any idea what you're talking about. I have commitments and need to go."

But the reporter wasn't giving up that easily. "Is there some reason you don't want to talk about the medical condition of Lissa or her father? Are you claiming doctor-patient privilege?"

"I'm not claiming anything," Karin snapped and looked around her. Damn. There were nothing but houses along here. If there was anything even remotely related to the festival, she would have claimed it needed her attention. She hurried her stride instead. "I don't have the slightest idea who or what you are talking about."

"Come on, Doctor. You expect me to believe that this Melissa McCarron is not the Melissa McCarron who's the Crunchy Flakes kid?"

Karin stared at the woman, her exasperation growing. "I never heard of Crunchy Flakes or the Crunchy Flakes kid."

The woman pulled some papers out of her pocket

and thrust them at Karin. "That's not your Melissa McCarron?"

Karin stopped walking and looked at the top paper. It was an ad for the cereal, featuring a little girl in overalls, curly light brown hair and the biggest, warmest brown eyes in creation. No, the second biggest and warmest. Jed had his daughter beat in that department.

Karin looked at the other papers. They were clippings from various newspapers, but all with the same photo accompanying a short article on the festival. The photo had been taken at the elementary school and showed a group of kids painting yellow bricks on the school sidewalk. Lissa—recognizably so—was front and center.

Karin wanted to deny that she'd ever seen this little girl before, but couldn't. Her newly discovered heart quivered slightly. How could she be hoping for a future between her and Jed when he didn't even care enough to share this truth about Lissa?

"She's a worldwide spokesperson for the cereal," Cooper said. "They feature her in all their television ads."

Karin shook her head slowly, her eyes still glued to the paper. "I hardly watch television, and if I do, I don't pay attention to the ads."

"I see," Cooper said. "You're engaged to Melissa's father, but didn't know she's a celebrity?"

Karin realized the photographer was still taking pictures. Something tightened up inside her, something turned cold and pushed the world away.

"I still don't see why any of this matters," she said.

"Because she was voted the most popular kid in America," Cooper said. "And if there's a rumor she's moving to Indiana just when her contract is up for renewal, her career could go down the tubes.''

"With your gentle help,'' Karin pointed out.

The reporter shrugged. "If she's a story, we have the right to tell it.''

"Well, she's not,'' Karin snapped. "She's just a kid on vacation.''

"She's not a story or she's not moving here?''

Karin frowned. If she walked away from this reporter, the woman would write the story anyway. But it would probably be filled with lies and innuendos. Lissa's career could be ruined either way. Well, not either way.

"There's no story,'' Karin said. "Wherever you got your information, it was wrong. Jed and Lissa are here on vacation, that's all. They'll be returning to Los Angeles tomorrow to resume Lissa's career.''

Cooper gave her a long look. "Is Jed McCarron the father of your child?''

Karin looked her straight in the eye. "No, he's not.''

Cooper's face fell, and she clicked off the tape recorder. "Damn.''

The photographer lowered the camera. "Now what?''

Cooper shrugged. "We do a story on America's most popular kid on vacation.''

"But you'll spoil her fun if you follow her around with a camera,'' Karin protested.

The reporter just looked at her. "You got a better story I can send in?'' she asked wearily. "This is a business, Doc. My editors sent me out here to get a story, I have to bring one back.''

She slipped her recorder into her pocket and nodded to the photographer. "Let's go find her.''

Karin stood still and watched them walk toward the festival area downtown. So Lissa was famous and Jed was a liar. No, she guessed he hadn't actually lied if one defined the word narrowly. He hadn't ever said to her that Lissa wasn't famous. He just hadn't ever told her she was.

Why? Had he thought he couldn't trust Karin to keep the secret? All he would have had to do was threaten to tell they weren't really engaged. Even if he hadn't trusted her, he should have known she wouldn't tell. No, he hadn't told for one simple reason—it hadn't mattered if she knew.

It was kind of funny, in a strange way. Here she had been sure she had no heart, and she finds out she did because she could feel it breaking.

Keeping her eye out for the *Worldwide News* crew, Karin walked through the crowd at the vendors' booths along Main Street. There were thousands of people looking at the *Wizard of Oz* memorabilia and the other crafts, but she didn't see the *Worldwide News* people or Jed and Lissa. She just hoped the reporter hadn't found them already. Karin had no idea how she felt about any of this, but she knew she had to warn Jed.

"Karin, hey. You look—" Heather stopped, a worried frown on her face. "What's the matter?"

Was it that obvious? She tried to smooth the worry lines away. "Nothing. I just can't find Jed and Lissa."

Heather's frown faded and she laughed. "Hey, a man that much in love can't be far away."

The words jabbed at her heart, needles trying to burst the little dream she'd been so foolishly building. But she had to hide the hurt under a smile. "Well, if you see him, would you tell him I need to talk to him?"

"Sure will." Heather started to walk past, then stopped. "Wait a minute. I do know where he is. Your mom said she sent him back to the bar to get her another roll of film."

"Maybe I can catch him there." Karin forced her smile to last a moment longer. "Thanks loads."

Actually, that would be great if he was in the bar, Karin thought and hurried down Morgan Street. It would mean they could talk undisturbed, though Karin had no idea what she was going to say to him. But what was there to say? All the hurt was because of fantasies she'd concocted, not because of anything he'd said or done. She would just warn him about the reporters, not bring up any of the rest of it.

When she went into the bar and found him on his way out, she forgot all her plans. All she knew was the pain so new, so strong, that she couldn't think of anything else.

"You lied to me," she cried. "You said you were a cowboy."

Jed stopped, looking confused. "I am."

"Oh, yeah. Right." Karin snorted. "And your daughter is just an ordinary little girl. Not some kind of worldwide spokesperson for a big cereal company."

"What's that got to do with anything?" He was acting confused.

"You didn't tell me."

"It never came up," he said. "And I don't see what difference it makes anyway."

Not see what difference it makes? The fact that he kept something so major from her didn't make a difference? That in itself was as hurtful as an outright lie would have been.

"It seems pretty odd that it never got mentioned," she said.

"There are lots of things that never got mentioned this past week."

But nothing so major. Nothing that anchored him so firmly in California. Nothing that made her stupid little dreams impossible.

"I suppose you're right," she said stiffly. "I'm making a fuss over nothing. Why, I didn't tell you that I usually use French dressing on my salads and you aren't fussing about that."

"Lissa being in cereal ads has nothing to do with anything," he snapped. "It didn't make any difference to anything we were doing here."

"No?"

"No." There was no doubt in his voice. "She wanted to be a regular kid on this vacation. She didn't want anyone fussing over her. So that's what we did. I didn't hurt anybody by going along with that wish."

Only a foolish woman who had learned about love the hard way. But that was a consequence to be hidden at all costs.

"Mom and I wouldn't have rushed around telling people, you know." She tried to keep the pain out of her voice. "We would have kept her secret."

"There was no reason to tell it. No one recognized her. There was no need to protect her."

As an argument, it would have worked with anyone he hadn't made love to. Anyone who hadn't shared her deepest fears with him. Anyone who hadn't found out she had a heart by falling in love with him.

But those were her problems and her way of seeing things. Obviously, none of those things had mattered to him.

"Well, you're wrong about no one recognizing her." Karin didn't even bother to hide the weariness in her voice. "A reporter approached me a few minutes ago. She wanted to interview me about you and Lissa. When she found out there was no story, she went looking for you both."

"Damn." A montage of emotions danced across his face. Anger, impatience, determination, decision. He clutched the box of film a bit tighter. "We're going to have to get out of here and quick. By dinner, reporters will be on this place like a swarm of locusts."

Karin froze up inside as he disappeared into the hall. She heard his steps on the stairs up to the apartment. That was it? Reporters were around, so it was goodbye Chesterton? It was what she had expected, but she had hoped for something else.

She turned and followed him upstairs. She found him in her mom's bedroom, packing up Lissa's things.

"She'll miss the rest of the festival," Karin said.

He shrugged. "It can't be helped. It's not that I really mind talking to a reporter, but once Lissa gets recognized, people converge on her. It's not safe without Crunchy Flake's security people to keep control."

"That doesn't seem like much of a life," she said.

He looked up at her, his eyes defensive, his jaw tight. He zipped the bag shut sharply. "It was her choice. All along," he pointed out. "She got into it on a whim and chose to stay. No one's forced her."

"Does she know that?"

"What's that supposed to mean?" he snapped and swung the bag off the bed. "That I'm subliminally making her stay in advertising? What kind of a father do you think I am?"

"How would I know?" she snapped back. "It's not like I know you."

His brown eyes were pools of turmoil. "No, you don't. Not any more than I know you. Lucky we kept it that way."

"It certainly is."

He turned and stomped into the other bedroom. *Their* room. She just stood still, frozen to the spot, with her eyes closed as she listened to the soft sounds of him packing his things. It hurt more than she had ever expected. The baby moved inside her, as if it was trying to keep him here, too, and somehow the pain was all that much greater.

What a fool she had been to let herself fall in love. She should never have started that stupid pretense. From the start she should have admitted the truth to her mother and friends. All she was left with was pain. She heard his steps coming back this way and she opened her eyes.

"I've got our things," he said. His eyes were shuttered and cool.

"Okay." She took a deep breath and tried to think beyond the pain. "Where's Lissa? Do you know?"

"She went to Ginger's."

Karin nodded. "What about a car? You can take mine if you want. You can leave it at the airport and I can get it later."

He shook his head. "They'd be watching for your car."

"How about Mom's then? She hardly uses it and it wouldn't be traced that easily."

He hesitated for a long moment, but finally nodded. "Okay. I'll call and let you know where we've left it."

"That's fine."

She went into the kitchen for the spare set of keys and handed them to him. Then there didn't seem to be much else to say.

"Good luck," she said.

He nodded. "Thanks. You, too. With the baby, I mean."

She nodded also, feeling like a dog looking out the back window of a car, just bobbing its head with the motion of the car.

"Well." He picked up the suitcases. "This is it then."

"Yep." Not much chance of a goodbye hug with his hands full of luggage. Just as well. She didn't want one anyway. She opened the back door for him.

He started out the door, but paused at her side. His eyes had softened but she couldn't read any message there. It was probably just the glare of the late-morning sun. A long moment passed, then another, but then he took a deep breath and went outside without a word.

She watched him go out on the porch, blinking back a sudden wetness in her eyes. She was not going to stand there and watch him go. The whole world would know how she felt then, and that was something nobody needed to know.

"I'm going back out the front way," she called after him. "Just in case someone was watching."

He turned, about to start down the steps. "Sure. Good thinking. Want to take that roll of film on the bar to your mom?"

"Glad to." How was her voice so bright and lively when her heart was dying? "So long."

"Bye."

She barely heard him as she closed the door. Maybe it would have been more polite to watch and wave from the door, but that was more than she was able to give. She took a deep breath that only increased the ache in her heart and walked slowly through the apartment.

In the living room, Shilah was sniffing at something on the floor under an end table, batting at it with a little paw.

"What's there, pussycat?" Karin asked. "You find a bug?"

But when Karin moved the cat aside and looked under the table, she found the little bunny rattle they'd gotten at the baby fair. Karin sank onto the floor, looking at the tiny toy and feeling the baby stir inside her.

She'd been wrong before when she'd thought that all she had left from Jed's visit was pain. He had given her a lot, if she wanted to be honest about it. He'd given her belief in herself and her ability to mother. Quite a gift, when she thought about it. Quite a magnificent gift.

Maybe there was a way to repay him. To give him a small gift in return. She scrambled to her feet and hurried to the door. She had to find Heather…and fast.

Jed drove the car down the alley where fewer people were walking. At every parking spot he passed, he had the urge to park and run back to see Karin. What the hell was the matter with him?

It was just that he had handled things so badly. He should have told her about Lissa, except that Chesterton seemed so far removed from Los Angeles, he felt as if he and Lissa were different people here. They could be whomever they wanted to be, and no one would care.

But he should have known better. Even if Lissa had been sucked into the role of being a regular kid, he shouldn't have forgotten that she wasn't. He should have been more on guard for the secret getting out. And he should have been watching out to make sure no one else got hurt. He hadn't watched out for Karin nearly well enough.

He stopped at a stop sign and waited for a giggling group of girls dressed as wicked witches to cross the street. They were safely across but he still didn't move. He had this nagging feeling he was forgetting something, that he was leaving something important behind, but a quick check in the back seat said he had three suitcases—which was all they came with.

It was leaving in a hurry that was causing his hesitation, he told himself, and drove across the intersection. If he didn't have time to think things out, he usually forgot something. But if he had left something behind, he could always ask Karin to send it.

Karin.

Just to say her name in his mind hurt. Damn, but he was going to miss her. She'd been a good sport about everything. Fun to argue with and even more fun to make up with. He hated like hell to leave her. He wondered if there was any chance she'd get offered a position at an L.A. hospital. Or if there was any chance she'd accept one if it was offered.

He stopped in front of Ginger's house and got out of the car, walking slowly up to the porch where Lissa was sitting as Ginger braided her hair.

"Hey, darlin'," he said.

She looked up. "Hi, Daddy. What are you doing here? I thought we were going to meet at Munchkinland."

"Something came up, darlin', and I need to talk to you."

Lissa frowned. "Dad, we're practicing for the play."

"It's important, Lissa."

The lights dimmed in Lissa's eyes. She knew something was wrong. Damn. He was messing this up.

She came over to him slowly and he led her over to the car where they could talk without Ginger overhearing.

"Lissa," he said softly and stooped so he was eye level with her. "Reporters know you're here in town. They're looking for us."

The light went out of her eyes. "What are we going to do?"

"Nothing much we can do but leave." He tried to make his voice softer to gentle the hard truth. "If we drive into Chicago, we can lose them pretty easy."

"But it's almost time for the play. Will we get back in time?"

His heart was about to break. She didn't understand. "We're not coming back, darlin.' We've got to go home."

She just looked at him, her eyes reflecting her disappointment. "But what about Karin and Grandma? And I promised Shilah I would brush her tonight after dinner when we watch television together."

"They'll understand. They'd want you to stay safe."

"But I don't want to go," she cried, her voice becoming a wail.

"We don't have a choice."

He pulled her into his arms and held her, feeling her disappointment in the air. This whole thing had gone wrong from start to finish. He should have insisted on Walt Disney World. They would have had a great time there, lots of fun and no hurt.

He loosened his hold on her. "Go back over and tell—"

Just then a car pulled up behind Marge's at the curb and he stiffened. Had they found him already? But it was only Heather jumping from the car.

"Thank goodness, I found you guys," she said, breathing hard as if she'd been running. "Come on, take my car and go on over to my house. We haven't got much time."

"Time for what?" Lissa asked.

Jed continued to hold Lissa's hand in his. "Actually, we were just on our way," he said. "Once Lissa's ready, we're going to be leaving."

Heather glanced around her. "Yeah, I know all about everything," she said. "Karin told me. She sent me here."

Karin sent her? "Why?"

"To fix things." She rolled her eyes in exasperation. "There isn't time to explain right now."

"There isn't time not to," Jed said. "Exactly what did she tell you?"

"Not much that we all didn't know already," Heather said, then turned toward the house. "Ginger, want to ask your mom to come out here? I need to ask her a favor."

"Okay," the girl said and ran into the house.

"Heather—"

She took a deep breath. "Okay. Quickly. Karin told me about Lissa being the Crunchy Flakes kid, which we all knew since some of us watch television on occasion."

"You knew?" Lissa asked, her voice almost breathless.

Heather smiled at her, then it turned to a frown.

"Hey, sugar. What happened to your braid?" She turned Lissa around and began to fix her hair. "Yes, we knew but we figured if you wanted to keep it secret, you must have a good reason."

"But...but..." Jed didn't know what to say.

"Some reporters are in town now," Lissa said and handed Heather a ribbon for the braid. "Daddy said we need to leave."

Heather tied the braid up, then gave Lissa a hug. "Leaving would be one solution, I guess. But Karin thought up a better one. One so you could stay in town and see the rest of the festival."

"How can we do that?" Jed asked, his heart leaping up with hope. It was just that he didn't like to see Lissa's vacation ruined. That was all. Seeing Karin again had nothing to do with it.

"Easy," Heather said. "Instead of dressing up like Dorothy and the Tinman, the town is going to dress up like Jed and Lissa."

Chapter Twelve

Lissa giggled. "Really?" she asked.

But Jed was dumbfounded. The town was going to dress up like him and Lissa? How in the world were they going to do that?

Heather handed him her car keys, and took his from his hand. "Go on over to my house and wait for me. I've got some planning to do with Ginger's mom, then I'll drive your car over. If someone saw you leave the bar, this will throw them off. You do remember where I live, don't you?"

"Yeah, but—"

Heather waved her hands, shooing them toward her car. "Get going. If this gets messed up, Karin will never forgive me."

But his feet wouldn't move. "Why is she doing this? I don't get it."

Heather just looked at him, then burst into laughter. "Why do you think, silly?"

"But you don't understand. Our relationship wasn't…" How could he put it? "What it seemed."

"I know all about the fake engagement," Heather said. "I told you she told me. Now, will you get going?"

"I gotta get my stuff," Lissa said and ran back to the porch. In a moment, she was running back to the car, her Dorothy dress, magic shoes and a small picnic basket in her arms.

Ginger's mom came outside. "What's going on?" she asked.

"Go," Heather ordered Jed, then hurried up to the porch herself.

Jed got Lissa into Heather's car, then climbed in. There didn't seem much point in arguing and, to be honest, he wasn't sure he wanted to. Heather's house was only a couple of blocks away, so minutes later he pulled into her driveway. The house looked quiet and still.

He turned off the engine and pulled the keys from the ignition. "I hope her house keys are here."

Lissa had opened her door, but stopped to give him a look. "Dad, this is Chesterton."

"I forgot." Chesterton, the land of the trusting. Leave your house open. Take in strangers. Trust them with all you hold precious.

For all her big-city ways, Karin was still a small-town girl and way too trusting. What if he'd taken advantage of her kindness? A little nagging voice pointed out that he had. And repaid her with hurt.

Jed took Lissa's hand and hurried up the walk.

Heather's husband, Alex, opened the door for them and waved them in as he talked into a cordless phone.

"That's right, blue jeans and a white shirt." Alex looked Jed over from toes to head, a frown on his face. "Medium blue. Washed-out look. What? Oh, okay. You aren't the only one. Gym shoes'll have to do. And girls should dress as Dorothy."

Alex broke the connection and smiled. "Come on in and sit down. There's stuff to eat or drink in the kitchen if you're hungry. I'd fix you something but I've a list of people to call. Just make yourselves at home."

"We're fine," Jed said and went into the living room as he heard Alex entering another number into the phone.

So that's how it was going to work. Other people were going to dress up like him and Lissa. He supposed it might work, but why would they bother? Why would the town go out of its way to do this for strangers?

Alex's voice drifted in. "Mickey? You heard? Yep, that's the routine…"

"Look, Daddy, a kitten," Lissa said. She sat down on the floor and tried to coax a little gray tabby cat out from under a chair. "Isn't it cute?"

"Yep." Jed sat down and picked up the newspaper. It was a local one, filled with Oz-festival stories and pictures. Filled with Karin. He stared at her picture until he could have sworn she smiled at him.

That's why the town was helping him and Lissa, he realized. For Karin. Because they loved her and thought he did too.

Lordy. He pulled off his hat and sat there, arms on his knees and hat in hand as he stared at the floor. What a mess this all was turning out to be. Just yesterday he'd been talking to Karin about his sense of honor, and today he was leading a whole town on. A whole generous town full of wonderful people. He was worse than a scoundrel.

A sound at the door woke him from his brooding. Heather was back and she was all smiles.

"It's going great," she said as she tossed her purse into a chair. "By the time the play starts this afternoon, you guys should be invisible."

"Like a ghost?" Lissa asked. "Cool."

Heather laughed. "Not exactly like that, but close."

He couldn't go through with this. "I really appreciate all that you're doing but—"

Alex came in from the kitchen, still holding the phone. "We've got a slight problem," he said. "Nobody has cowboy boots. The jeans and shirt are easy, and Marge has more hats than we have heads in town, but hardly any of the men in town have cowboy boots."

Heather's face turned serious as she turned toward Jed. "Guess we have to find you another kind of footwear," she said. "What's your preference? Athletic shoes or work boots?"

"Maybe we should forget all this," he said.

"Daddy can't wear some other kind of shoes," Lissa said. "Cowboys always wear their boots."

Jed put his arm around her shoulders. "No, it's not that, honey. It's not fair to make everyone go to so much trouble for us."

"Trouble schmubble," Heather said and turned to Alex. "Go with gym shoes. We'll find Jed a pair."

Didn't anyone in this town listen? Jed got to his feet. "I meant what I said. This is too much."

Heather did stop then, but just shook her head. "We want to do it. You both mean a lot to us."

"But—" Jed stopped.

Lissa was watching him, her heart in her eyes. She wanted this vacation so much. Letting the town hide them would mean she'd get to stay for the whole festival. Did he have the right to deny her that?

He tried to concentrate on that fact, but all his mixed-up mind kept telling him was that, if they stayed, he'd see Karin again.

Toto took off his cowboy hat and waved the audience back with it. "Let's not crowd the stage, folks. If we stay back, everybody can see."

Satisfied that the audience was going to stay behind the portable barricades, he went back to his place off to the side of the flatbed truck being used as a stage. Up on it, Mickey Juarez was narrating the story of *The Wizard of Oz,* while costumed volunteers ad-libbed their way through a scene with the Flying Monkeys.

"Those hats come in handy, don't they?" Karin whispered to Toto.

"I don't feel like myself in it though," he said. "Or this getup. I should be in uniform."

"I think you look very handsome," Karin told him with a smile.

Toto glowered at her, good witch that she was dressed up to be, and went back to watching the crowd. It was the weirdest thing, looking out over the people watching the *Wizard of Oz* production and seeing at least a hundred cowboys. A hundred Dorothys was no big deal, they got that and more each year. But all those cowboys was sure an oddity.

"How many cowboy hats did your mother have anyway?" he asked Karin. "I could swear she didn't have this many."

"She didn't," she said. "Once Heather and everybody started making calls, they found out lots of people had one they could use."

"Huh." He looked out at the crowd again, wondering if the reporter was still around or not. Didn't matter either way. He'd bet she'd never find Jed or Lissa. "Guess it worked out pretty good, didn't it?"

Karin didn't answer him for a moment and he turned back to her. Maybe she hadn't heard him over the clapping of the crowd, but he could tell by the shadow in her eyes that she had.

"Yes, it worked out wonderfully," she said. Her voice was filled with forced emotion. "Just as perfectly as I had hoped."

"Why do I think you're lying?" Toto asked. "If you don't like what's happening, do something about it."

"You're a fine one to talk," she said. "When do you plan on doing something about you and Dorothy?"

"What's there to do? She's happy with things the way they are."

"Is she?" The clapping stopped and Karin turned toward the stage. "Oops, that's my cue. At last I get to be in a scene."

While he watched, she climbed up the stairs on the side of the stage and walked up to the front to announce the next scene's location. Then she drew the numbers of the volunteers who would get to play characters in the final scene.

"Dorothy will be played by Dorothy number 87," Karin said and a squeal went up on the far side of the crowd.

"You don't go in for costumes?" someone asked Toto.

He turned and found Jed at his side. A Lissa-sized Dorothy was nearby with three other Dorothys, all dressed nearly the same as the hundred or so other Dorothys in the crowd.

"You don't call this a costume?" Toto asked, waving at the cowboy clothes he was wearing. "I feel like I'm ten and it's Halloween."

"You're missing a trick-or-treat bag though."

"Never did bother with them," Toto admitted. "Just ate as I went. Saved a lot of time and trouble."

"Ah," Jed said with a nod. "A man of efficiency."

"The Scarecrow will be played by Scarecrow number 22," Karin went on.

Toto could feel Jed's mood change and his attention shift to the stage.

"She's a mighty fine woman, isn't she?" Jed said quietly.

Toto nodded. "One of the best." Not Dorothy, but then no one else was or would be for him.

"Why the hell did she do all this? We had a fight. I didn't mean to, but I really hurt her. So why was she willing to fix it so we could stay?"

Toto didn't like to get involved with other people's relationships. He figured he had enough trouble making sense of his heart, without trying to understand someone else's. Still, there was something in Jed's voice that said the question needed answering.

"Guess she forgave you," Toto said.

Jed stared at him as if he'd spoken in a foreign language. Maybe Toto had made a mistake. Maybe Jed hadn't wanted honesty, however apparent it was. Maybe he'd wanted a joke or some kind of guy ribbing that didn't say anything at all. Toto glanced at Jed's new, white athletic shoes.

"Maybe she wanted to see if she could get you to wear something else on your feet," Toto said with a quick laugh. "You know, see if she could change you from a cowboy to something else."

But his joke didn't bring the smile that Toto had been hoping for. Instead, Jed just stared down at his feet.

"I'm not a cowboy anymore, am I?" he muttered.

"Sure you are. You just aren't wearing boots." Jeez, everything he was saying came out wrong today. He looked up at the stage in relief. "Hey, Karin's done announcing the cast for the final scene. I've got to move everybody over to the last set. I'll see you over there."

"Yeah, sure."

Jed's voice was distracted, but Toto just nodded and went to work, directing the crowd to Glinda's castle set in the schoolyard. The flatbed truck moved slowly along and once in place, then the audience gathered around it while the cast assembled. Toto took his place at one side to help maintain order, but turned to watch the production.

Funny, Dorothy was playing Dorothy in the scene. It wasn't the first time her number had been picked for a scene, but there was something bothersome about her playing the part in this particular one, the one where Dorothy finds the way to leave Oz and go back home.

While Mickey explained the background for the scene, Dorothy, Karin and a few other townsfolk arranged themselves on the stage. Then Mickey stepped back to let the characters tell the story.

Dorothy and her friends arrived at Glinda's castle, making small talk among themselves. Nothing exciting, but it generated a few laughs from the audience. Toto smiled too. Then some teenage boy, playing a castle guard, asked the travelers to state their business.

"I want to find my way home," Dorothy proclaimed.

The words nipped at Toto's heart, but nothing he couldn't handle. He did turn slightly though so that he was watching the crowd more. That's what he was supposed to be doing anyway, not ogling Dorothy.

"But don't you like it in Oz?" Glinda asked Dorothy, up on the stage.

Dorothy shrugged. "It's nice, but it's not where I belong."

Toto turned completely away. He didn't need to hear this. He knew that she felt she didn't belong in Chesterton, he didn't need to hear her say it to hundreds of people.

"But isn't it more exciting here?" Glinda persisted.

"Excitement isn't everything," Dorothy said, her voice sounding puzzled as if Karin was straying from the normal line of conversation. "Kansas is home. Can't you help me get back there?"

Toto twisted his lips as he looked at the crowd. He didn't need to be here at all. This was crazy. There were other officers around working crowd control. He should go over to the security headquarters and see if there was something else he should be doing. See if there were any reports of trouble around. He started to work his way through the crowd.

"Thomas Tollinger, come back here!" Karin ordered from up on the stage.

He turned. The play had apparently stopped. Karin was at the front of the stage, arms akimbo, as she glared down at him. Everyone, both on the stage and off, was staring at her. Or staring at him.

"I have to go check in at the security tent," he told her.

"You do not," she snapped. "You're running away again. Every time Dorothy starts talking about how unhappy she is in Paris, you run away."

"I never said that!" Dorothy cried.

"Hey, she loves it in Paris," a teenage Dorothy in the audience argued.

"It's wonderful," another cried.

"Magical."

Karin frowned at them all, looking like a schoolmarm with a classful of juvenile delinquents. A schoolmarm in pink ruffles with a glittery crown and a magic wand, but still a schoolmarm.

"She does not," Karin said, slowly and carefully. "It may be a wonderful, magical place to visit, but it's not home." She turned to include the real Dorothy in her glare. "Right?"

Dorothy shrugged uneasily. "I probably haven't given it enough time," she said. "I'm expecting too much too fast."

"Maybe you miss your friends," Karin suggested.

"I can still keep in touch, and I can make new ones," Dorothy said.

But there was something in her voice that Toto hadn't heard before. An uncertainty. He took a step forward.

"I've met lots of really nice people there," Dorothy went on.

"It still might not be where you belong," Karin said more softly.

Dorothy's chin went up in what Toto knew was a sign of embarrassment. "I saved for years to go."

"She was following her dreams," an audience Dorothy called out.

"Dreams can take you all sorts of places and bring you back again," Karin said. "Dreams can change. Maybe it's time she followed her heart." She gave Dorothy a hug before looking back out at the audience. At Toto. "Maybe it's time someone else followed his heart, too."

But Toto was barely listening to her. His feet were taking him up to the stage steps though he didn't remember telling them to. All he could see, all he could think about was Dorothy and that uncertainty in her voice. Suddenly a million little things had new meanings, wonderful new meanings. Maybe he and Junior didn't have to live alone.

Then he was on the stage and Dorothy was there facing him. He felt as if his heart had climbed into his mouth, and he'd never be able to speak. But she held out her hand, just a little, ever so tentatively, and he went forward to take it. And then, since he had her hand anyway, he pulled all the rest of her into his embrace.

"Don't go back to Paris, Dorothy," he said. "Stay here. I love you. I've loved you for years. I can make you happier than Paris can."

"Toto!" she cried and threw her arms around his neck.

Their kiss was an explosion of love and longing and passion too long denied. His arms could not hold her tight enough, his lips could not taste her deeply enough. There were years of loneliness to erase and years of love ahead and every moment with her in his arms was a pledge of that.

Karin laughed. "I think Dorothy's found her way back home."

The audience laughed, then clapped, and Toto slowly loosened his hold on Dorothy. But only slightly. He was not letting go of her again.

"Come on, Susie. Mavis. Jeremy. Get in closer to Glinda," the woman said from behind her camera.

Karin held her smile in place as the little kids crowded in closer around the thronelike chair she was sitting in. This was the last event of the day—the chance for the kids to come talk to her and have their picture taken with Glinda. She didn't mind it really, but she did wish it was time to go home. All this smiling was wearing her out. This wonderful heart that she'd recently discovered she had was pretty weary and wanted to be alone.

"Now, thank Glinda, children," the woman said.

"Thanks," the kids said in unison. "Thanks a lot."

"Sure," she told them.

They hurried off with their mother to get in line to be photographed with Elmer as the Wizard. Karin smiled at the next group of kids coming up into the Emerald City set at the train station. Night had fallen so it was dark all around the set, but lights had been placed to shine on the platforms for the pictures. It made it as bright as day up here, but she had no idea how many more people were waiting in line.

"Can I interest you in a glass of lemonade?" someone said behind her.

Karin turned. "Penny!" she cried and jumped to her feet to hug her friend tightly. "How was the honeymoon? When did you get back?"

"Great and this morning." Penny gingerly extricated

herself, and handed Karin the glass of lemonade. "We couldn't miss your moment of glory. Where's Jed?"

Karin's excitement vanished in the blink of an eye. She took the glass with concentrated interest, and had a long sip of the lemonade. "Oh, he's around someplace." She turned to smile at the two little boys waiting their turn and handed the glass back to Penny without really looking her way. "Hi, kids. Want to have your picture taken?"

The boys stood on either side of her while their dad took the picture. He took forever to focus the camera and then didn't like the way the kids were arranged, but Karin didn't care. The longer, the better, as far as she was concerned. She was in no hurry to explain this whole crazy week to Penny.

And as for where Jed was, Karin had no idea. She had seen him briefly during the play and not at all since then. The place was filled with Jed look-alikes, but she hadn't been fooled for a second by them. Maybe the reporter hadn't either. Maybe it had been a stupid idea and Jed and Lissa had had to leave anyway. Or maybe Jed chose to leave, tired of the whole mess. She hadn't seen Lissa for ages either. The girl had never had the chance to ask Glinda her big question.

The picture was finally taken and the boys stepped away. "Thanks," the father said and led his two off the platform. Karin sighed and adjusted her crown. It felt as if it was slipping.

"I heard about your make-believe relationship with Jed," Penny said. "Your plan was just brilliant. I always knew you were. That's why I always wanted you to skip school with us. You would have figured out ways to insure we were never caught."

"I wouldn't bet on it," Karin said, turning to talk to her friend. "The way things go for me—"

"Oops, this is where I go find someone else to talk to," Penny said.

Karin turned back, expecting to see another group of kids coming up to have their picture taken. Instead, she saw Jed. Her heart took a leap upward, but he looked so serious that it came crashing back down.

Maybe he was coming to tell her it was over—but it had never started, so how could that be?

Maybe he was coming to tell her that he and Lissa were leaving—but they had already said goodbye so that was hardly necessary.

Maybe he was coming to tell her that he loved her and never wanted to go. Yeah, right, and once she got done hearing that, she was going to go write a letter to the Easter Bunny.

She realized he had a small box in his hand and her heart sank even further. He was bringing her a hostess gift. A duty present to the person who gave you room and board for the week. She would have rather he'd left in anger than treated her with cool and distant courtesy.

Though her knees felt wobbly, she got to her feet. Bad news was better taken standing.

"Hello, Jed."

He stopped in front of her. "Hello, darlin'," he said softly.

Her knees went even wobblier, if that was possible, but her head told her not to be an idiot. This "darlin'" was no different from any other "darlin'" he'd called her over the past week. She was letting her imagination run wild.

"Did the reporter ever find you and Lissa?" She

could hear the buzz of people walking around below her and saw the flash of cameras, and told herself she could do this. She could talk to Jed calmly and quietly, and not give her feelings away. This was just part of playing Glinda.

"Nope, your plan worked just fine," he said. "I saw the newspaper people leaving town after the Munchkin dinner, so we should be safe."

"I'm so glad," she said. Her voice quivered a bit this time. Maybe her control wasn't quite as strong. She clutched her magic wand a little tighter and remembered people were watching her. "You must be happy."

He pushed his hat back on his head. "No, darlin', actually I'm not," he said. "I have to say I'm about as far from happy as I've been for a long time."

Her stomach tightened with worry. Had she done something? What in the world could he be upset about? But she was facing into the lights so his face was in the shadows. She couldn't see his eyes to read anything in them.

"I'm sorry. I'd hoped you would enjoy your stay in town."

"Well, the truth is, I've lost a few things and it's made my stay kind of unsatisfying."

He lost some things? This wasn't what she expected at all. Somehow the mundaneness of the idea caused the ache in her heart to double. Her throat hurt and talking was agony. Or was it just being near him and not having him care that hurt so?

"Have you checked with Toto?" she asked. "They keep a lost and found at the police station."

He shook his head slowly. "These aren't exactly things I put down someplace by mistake," he said.

''Though I was hoping that you could help me get one of the things back.''

''Me? Of course, whatever I can do.''

He took off his hat then, slipping the package he was holding under his arm so that he could hold his hat in both hands before him. She still couldn't see his eyes, but she could feel something change in the air around them. Her nerves were suddenly on edge with a fragile hope.

''You can make an honest man of me.''

She was confused. ''I can what?''

''Make an honest man of me.'' He took a deep breath and went on. ''You see, a cowboy doesn't lie. He's a man of honor. Yet this whole week I've been living a lie.''

Her hope was drying up. ''I'm not sure I understand.'' Her voice was raw. ''You want me to confess to the town that I made up our engagement?''

''Not at all, darlin','' he said. ''I'd like for you to marry me.''

The words seemed to echo around them, hovering there to mock and torment. Her heart stopped, went totally dead, and she just stared at him. She couldn't have heard him right, and if she did, he had to mean something other than what she thought.

''Marry you?'' she whispered.

He nodded. ''That way it won't have been a lie, you see. I can be a real cowboy again and not one living with dishonor.''

Her heart was in no hurry to start again, not when his reasons were as dumb as that. ''This sounds like some stupid macho thing,'' she said. She was desperately in love and he was talking about cowboy honor.

"You don't marry someone just because you told a lie earlier."

"No, not normally," he agreed. "But that brings me to the other thing I lost this weekend. My heart."

She stopped, her mouth partially open as she was ready to fight some more, to lash out at him for mocking her dreams. But his gentle voice froze her. She couldn't breathe and her eyes filled with tears. Putting her hands to her face as if that could hold in the fears and hopes and wonderful dreams that wanted to spill out into her voice, she looked at him.

"What are you saying?" Her voice sounded strangled and tight.

He let go of his hat with one hand and took her right hand down from her face, holding it tightly. "I'm saying I love you. I know you don't think you have a heart, but you do. You've got mine. And I'm quite happy to let you have it, if you would just let me stay here with you."

"But...but..." She didn't know what to say. Tears spilled over her cheeks. "But you can't love me."

He pulled her into his arms, wrapping her up tightly in a promise that he would never let her go. "Oh, but I do. I love you so much that it hurts. I love you so much that I was willing to wear these yuppie shoes instead of my boots just so I could stay here a little while longer."

They both looked down at his athletic shoes, then back at each other. She felt the smile in her heart move to her lips.

"That's quite a sacrifice," she said. "A real proof of love, but if the reporter left hours ago, you could have changed back."

He shook his head. "I was busy looking for these." He handed her the small box he'd brought with him.

She didn't want to let go of him, but had to open the box. Hands trembling, she untied the golden ribbon keeping it closed and took off the lid. Inside was a pair of cowboy boots. A pair of baby-sized cowboy boots. She stared at them, wondering how her heart could feel as if it was breaking when she was so happy.

"Oh, Jed," she said with a sigh.

"They're for our baby," he said and put his hand possessively over her stomach. His other arm was still around her shoulders. "Girl or boy, it's going to be a little cowpoke."

"They're wonderful."

"Does this mean you're going to marry me?" He tightened his hold on her.

Happy as she was, she still had worries crowding in. Had he really thought this through? "Where will we live?" she asked.

"What's wrong with right here?"

"But what about Lissa's career?"

He turned her to face him, both his arms encircling her. "I can take her to Los Angeles for ads, or they've got photographers in Chicago, too. She's thinking of giving it up though, so I don't think it's going to be an issue."

Slowly her worries were being eased away and happiness was sprouting up strong and tall. A smile crept into her voice. "Will you let me buy you a horse farm?"

His arms tightened even more. "We can buy a home for our family," he said, stressing the "we."

"And we'll raise the best horses in the area while we raise a family. But we'll have to talk about it all later. We've got a lot to do before the wedding tomorrow.''

She pulled back and stared up into his face. ''Tomorrow?''

''Why not?'' he said. ''Glinda marries her cowboy, isn't that the way the story ends?''

She just laughed. ''I love you so much,'' she said.

''Can you forgive me for not telling you about Lissa?'' Jed asked. ''It wasn't you I didn't trust. It was me. I didn't trust myself to not love you if I let you close.''

''Sweet Jed,'' Karin said softly. ''It's okay.'' She reached up to press her lips to his.

It was the kiss of a lifetime, and the promise of even more to come. Her heart was ready to burst, she was so happy, yet as his mouth took hers and his arms held her safe and close, she knew that this was only the beginning of happiness, only the lower reaches of the ecstasy that their life would be together.

She held him close and let his lips sing of his love to her soul. His hands promised protection and safety and the joy of being one. His arms vowed to hold her forever close and each day would be more wonderful than the one before.

When they finally broke apart for air, she heard the sound of applause from the people walking around Emerald City. She lay in his arms, not embarrassed at all and too happy to move. A sudden thought made her pull away and frown at him.

''What about Lissa?'' she asked. ''I thought she came here because she had a question for Glinda, but she's never asked me one.''

''I didn't have to,'' Lissa said.

Karin looked around Jed, and there was his daughter

skipping over. Her face was wreathed in smiles. Karin didn't have to wonder how she felt about all this. The girl climbed into the thronelike chair Karin had been seated in for the photographs.

"I wanted to ask Glinda how to make our house a home again, because it wasn't the same after Mommy died," Lissa told Karin, and grinned at them both. "But I don't need to ask that anymore."

"No, I don't think you do," Jed agreed. Karin had turned to face Lissa, but he'd kept both his arms around her. He brushed the side of her neck with his lips. "I think we've got all we need for a home again."

"But I've got another question for Karin." She looked Karin in the eye. "After you and Daddy get married, can I have a cat of my own?"

Karin broke free of Jed's arms to hug Lissa, her soon-to-be daughter. "You betcha," she said. "Our horse farm will be the perfect place for all sorts of pets."

"Oh, thanks so much, Karin." Lissa hugged her tight, then bounced away as if she had too much energy to stay still. "Just wait until I tell Ginger that I'm going to get a mom, and a baby brother or sister, and a cat and a horse farm. This is too cool."

She ran to the edge of the platform and skipped down the stairs as Karin and Jed watched. Then Karin turned to smile at Jed.

"I think I'd better get back to posing for pictures," she said.

"I was the last one in line. You're through for now."

"Am I?" She slid back into his arms. "Want Glinda to tell you how to get home then?"

He just held her closer, planting his lips on her hair. "She doesn't need to. Wherever you are is home for me. Now and for always."

Epilogue

"The baby's not due for another two weeks," Karin cried.

"Guess it's as impatient as its mama," Jed said. "Just hang on. We're almost to the hospital."

Another contraction came, hard and long. For a moment, Karin thought the wail in the air was from her, but then she realized Toto had turned on the police car's siren. Probably just as well. There was no doubt the baby was coming fast. The pain passed and Karin opened her eyes. Dorothy, so beautiful in her winter-white wedding dress, was looking worried.

"I am so sorry, Dorothy," she told her friend. "I told you not to have me be your matron of honor. But Penny or Heather could have stepped in. You shouldn't be postponing your wedding for this."

"Are you kidding?" Dorothy said. "We wouldn't be together if it wasn't for you."

"Besides, it's not like we aren't getting married," Toto said. "We're just changing the location a little."

"This is crazy," Karin said, then gripped Jed's hand as another contraction gripped her.

"Breathe," Jed said softly as he held her. "Remember to breathe."

She nodded and concentrated on that until the spasm passed. She was trembling slightly, a reaction to the pain and also a sudden return of her old worries. But then Jed was there, brushing the hair back from her face, one hand holding hers tightly as if he knew her fears. Just the way he was always there for her when she was tired or worried over a patient.

She smiled at him and the fears vanished. "This kid's sure in a hurry," she said.

"Maybe he's anxious to go square dancing," Dorothy suggested.

They all started to laugh, but the laugh turned into a contraction and Karin bore down again just as Toto pulled into the emergency-room driveway. In a moment, hands were helping her out of the car and onto a gurney. People were rushing around her, the pain was coming and going, and for a moment she was lost.

Then Jed was at her side, holding her hand as though he'd never let her go and letting his eyes tell her everything was going to be all right. They were swept away into a delivery room. She couldn't keep track of the contractions or the timing or who was there and who wasn't. All she knew was that Jed never left her side, and gave her the strength and courage to push that one last time and a squawling filled the air.

"It's a boy," Jed cried. "We have a little boy."

His voice broke with the love and happiness that filled it as he placed their son in her arms. She just looked at the baby and then at Jed and knew she was the luckiest woman on earth. Jed brushed her lips with his, but it was the look in his eyes that told her how much he loved her, loved them both.

Then Lissa was there to see her new brother and Karin's mother wanted to hold her grandson, and her world of love just seemed to grow and multiply. After a short time for Karin and the baby to get cleaned up and checked over, Penny and Brad were there oohing and aahing over the baby, maybe with a special tenderness since Penny was going to have their child in the summer. Heather and Alex were all smiles too; their baby was due a month before Penny's. Dorothy announced that Karin's baby would boss all of the others around, just as Karin had bossed them around, and Toto looked at Dorothy with such love and delight that Karin wondered if they, too, were starting a family.

"What's his name?" Lissa asked.

Karin turned back and took Jed's hand. "We want to name him Henry after Jed's grandfather."

"Hank," Marge said. "That's so nice. It's a good cowboy name."

In the middle of the laughter, there was a knock at the door and Elmer Brinkley stuck his head in. "Is this the place?"

"At last," Karin cried. "Come on in, Judge Brinkley. Don't you have a wedding to perform?"

"I've got the flowers," Lissa said, handing Dorothy her bouquet.

"I've got the rings," Jed said, patting his pocket.

The judge came in, followed by about a dozen more guests. Friends, relatives. The room was packed, but Karin couldn't have been more pleased. She held little Hank close, and kept Jed's hand still in hers.

''So if the bride and groom are ready,'' Elmer was saying, waving Dorothy and Toto over next to the bed. ''Let's get you near your matron of honor and your best man. There you go.'' He paused, then began. ''Dearly beloved…''

Karin sighed softly and thought how right that was. She looked around the room, her gaze gliding lovingly over her friends, her family, her newborn son, and stopping at Jed.

How lucky they all were. They all were beloved.

*   *   *   *   *

Silhouette Stars

Born this Month

Bryan Adams, Joan Sutherland, Richard Burton,
Demi Moore, Prince Charles, Meg Ryan, Boris Becker,
Jodie Foster, Calvin Klein

Star of the Month

Scorpio

An interesting year lies ahead, there could be
some major changes occurring especially in the
second half and although you may feel
apprehensive the outcome will be positive.
Romantically this is an excellent time and you
should find out just how strongly those around
you feel about you.

SILH/HR/0011a

 **Sagittarius**

Career matters are highlighted and you should feel pleased with the options on offer. A shopping spree mid-month could produce some real bargains.

Capricorn

The recent hectic social whirl slows down and you can take time out to recharge. A relationship that has given you concern seems at last to be on firm ground.

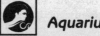 **Aquarius**

Family matters occupy your time and you could feel torn in several directions as those close refuse to take responsibility for their actions. However, late in the month the tension should start to fade and you will see a happier time approaching.

Pisces

A short break away from the routine will bring the romance back into your life. Finances look good and you may indulge in a little more than window shopping.

 Aries

Time to think about changing your environment either by moving home or planning some improvements. Your artistic talents will be working well and others will be impressed by your efforts.

Taurus

Recent financial gains have taken the pressure off and allowed you to make a few much needed changes in your life. This is the ideal time for new relationships or for making a stronger commitment to that special person.

SILH/HR/0011c

Gemini

Your faith in those around has been shaken and you are unsure about who exactly to trust. Remember not to assume everyone is the same as you as you'll find you have some very good friends. A party late in the month gets you in the mood for socialising.

Cancer

Romance is in the air and may come from an unexpected direction. Socially too it's a happy time and someone close may have a good reason to celebrate.

Leo

You may have reached the end of the road with a relationship but don't allow your disappointment to stop you seeing the other good aspects that are happening, especially in the workplace.

Virgo

Travel is well aspected especially when related to work where it could lead to some new openings. Romance should continue to go well as long as you are careful to include those close in your plans.

Libra

An interesting month in which you may feel the aspects are working against you. However, you can turn it around by seeing the positive side and being open to the suggestions made to you.

© Harlequin Mills & Boon Ltd 2000

Look out for more Silhouette Stars next month

FREE!

2 Books
and a surprise gift!

We would like to take this opportunity to thank you for reading this Silhouette® book by offering you the chance to take TWO more specially selected titles from the Special Edition™ series absolutely FREE! We're also making this offer to introduce you to the benefits of the Reader Service™—

- ★ FREE home delivery
- ★ FREE gifts and competitions
- ★ FREE monthly Newsletter
- ★ Books available before they're in the shops
- ★ Exclusive Reader Service discounts

Accepting these FREE books and gift places you under no obligation to buy; you may cancel at any time, even after receiving your free shipment. Simply complete your details below and return the entire page to the address below. *You don't even need a stamp!*

YES! Please send me 2 free Special Edition books and a surprise gift. I understand that unless you hear from me, I will receive 4 superb new titles every month for just £2.70 each, postage and packing free. I am under no obligation to purchase any books and may cancel my subscription at any time. The free books and gift will be mine to keep in any case.

E0ZEB

Ms/Mrs/Miss/Mr ....Initials...........................
BLOCK CAPITALS PLEASE

Surname..

Address..

....

....Postcode ....

Send this whole page to:
UK: The Reader Service, FREEPOST CN81, Croydon, CR9 3WZ
EIRE: The Reader Service, PO Box 4546, Kilcock, County Kildare (stamp required)

Offer not valid to current Reader Service subscribers to this series. We reserve the right to refuse an application and applicants must be aged 18 years or over. Only one application per household. Terms and prices subject to change without notice. Offer expires 31st May 2001. As a result of this application, you may receive further offers from Harlequin Mills & Boon Limited and other carefully selected companies. If you would prefer not to share in this opportunity please write to The Data Manager at the address above.

Silhouette® is a registered trademark used under license.

Special Edition™ is being used as a trademark.